D1649712

So She Wrote a Book

A. Maksimow

Copyright © 2021 A. Maksimow
All rights reserved
First Edition

Fulton Books, Inc.
Meadville, PA

Published by Fulton Books 2021

ISBN 978-1-63860-584-3 (paperback)
ISBN 978-1-63860-585-0 (digital)

Printed in the United States of America

To a dear childhood friend of
forty-plus years, Jane Caruso Malone.

Acknowledgments

It was only over the beginning of a hard work week, great conversation, and a glass of wine when my dear friend motived me to write this book. I had just returned from an emotional visit to the Florida area leaving my one and only dear son behind at college when my phone rang. My phone rang often, but it wasn't often I took a call from my busy friend Jane. Jane juggled a busy life as a mom of three and a wife of ten-plus years with a career. Having been through so much together since we were children and later, moms with children of our own, it was an important conversation to share. We shared many laughs in our conversation, as we always did, but this conversation was special. Not only did we reminisce through laughter, but we also shared tears in this conversation.

My dear friend, Jane, and I shared a moment of which I will never forget. I could visualize Jane's tears running down her face as her voice cracked all the same while I shed my very own tears. I had finished up sharing the story of my first goodbye to my precious Jake at college. It was as if mine and Jane's emotions and thoughts were aligned and in sync at that very same moment together. I felt we shared the very same thoughts in our mind of our boys gaining their independence. Our boys were becoming men, and I could feel the connection and love both Jane and I shared for our boys at that very moment through the phone. Our boys were finally grown up and off to begin a new chapter in their life! We loved them all so much throughout the years, but it was that moment when I knew our love for our boys had grown deeper and stronger than ever! It was a moment when I realized my special love for Jane, and the connection we shared had grown and expanded to a stronger love for each other's boys.

Friends and family asked how I would spend my time since I no longer had a child to care for in my home. I thought I may take up a new hobby like scuba dive or learn a new skill or even brush up on a foreign language. Of course, I thought of how I could continue the act of self-improvement. Ideas and thoughts of spending more time with the little children so they knew how truly loved they were also crossed my mind. I tossed around the thought of how I could help someone in need of a little hope or even just to brighten their day to let them know if it would all be okay. Jane, too, asked me what I would do with the extra time I would have on my hands while Jake was in college. It was at that very moment when Jane suggested I write a book since she felt my life intriguing, filled with both adventures and challenges. Jane suggested I write a book to inspire others and give others insight on how to overcome some of life's many challenges. Jane thought I had so much to share with the world through my many personal, real-life experiences. Not sure if was a total coincidence or if our lives are meant to sync and circle back, but I shared with her in our conversation that I actually started writing several years ago when my son was a toddler. My writing in the story was based on a true story that I never completed. My writing in my story was still untold, so maybe the better time to share this story was now! Jane inspired me once again to begin writing this story fifteen years later.

Thank you, Jane! You were such a large part of my childhood, and you will forever hold a special place in my heart.

Thank you!

I want to express much gratitude to those special friends and family who supported me through my personal journey in life. My parents stood by my side through thick and thin. Both my sisters and my niece will hold close positions to my heart—always and forever! Special love to Michelle and Danielle. You are both more beautiful and loved than you will ever know! The children are all so dear to me and precious.

For the rest of you (too many special people out there to mention), it's special people like you who inspire me to write my thoughts to share and spread the power of many forms of love all around us. My heart is with each and every one of you especially those that may have felt unloved in this world. Each and every one of us is loved.

Contents

Chapter 1

The First Cut Is the Deepest

As a little girl, I felt alone and disconnected from the people around me. I couldn't relate to my family, and I almost felt as if I belonged to another family somewhere else. My belonging was someplace in a more American home with a loving mom who spoke English and a protective dad without a heavy accent. I envisioned life with older siblings whom I could aspire to be like and, last but not least, a furry pet to cuddle with at night. I thought older siblings were supposed to be admired and look out for the youngest in the family. I felt I should live in more of a conservative home where there were rules and set guidelines. I thought school and work topics were supposed to be discussed at the dinner table and where family problems were solved. I thought parents were supposed to guide their children and discuss education, career, and preparation for our future over dinner at the dining table. I pictured myself raised in a home where Dad worked as the provider and Mom worked part-time out of the home and full time inside the home.

These thoughts and visions of how a home should be kept often crossed my mind as a young girl, but it was not my reality. I couldn't understand why other family homes were structured but mine was the farthest from it. I envisioned a neighborhood where neighbors were helpful and family and friends were welcome. Oh, how I desperately wanted to invite a friend over to play dolls in my private room where it was peaceful and quiet, but I just couldn't. I lived my days hidden with my sister Lina. I envisioned my room to be pink with pretty dolls and bows everywhere with plush thick carpet. I loved to play dress-up with pretty dolls, but I didn't own many of my own at all. I often thought how lucky our neighborhood friend was to own her own dollhouse the size of an actual shed filled with hundreds of dolls and cabbage babies. Lina and I were thrilled when our neighbor would invite us over to play dollhouse because it was a way to escape our environment.

I yearned for the English language to be spoken as the first language so I could ask my parents for help with my homework, but there was no one around to ask. I often teared up when I couldn't understand my homework, but I didn't want anyone to find me crying because I was too shy and embarrassed to talk about my feelings. I cried because I often felt alone and confused. At times, I would lose concentration in class because I was worried about my mom's safety.

I cried until my tears ran dry in the back seat of my dad's car. Oh no! We stopped again on the side of the main highway driving back from a family party. My dad stopped the car and dragged my beautiful, platinum blonde-haired mother out of the car by her neck. Dad held Mom forcefully over the ledge of a huge cliff off the side of a major highway, ready to push her over. I couldn't make out what my dad was yelling about. Lina was too scared and speechless to move.

I got out of the car in tears and shouted, "Please don't hurt my mommy. Please! Please don't!"

My beautiful mother's midnight-blue eye makeup ran down her face as she teared up from all the pain my dad caused her.

The pressures were all too much to manage for me as a little girl so I broke out with cold sores very often. I could barely eat from all the pain around my mouth. I lived in fear and worry most of my early childhood. I was a shy and quiet little girl with not much to talk about, and I always felt different than the other members of my family. One of the reasons may have been as a result of the fifteen-year age difference between the oldest sis and me. Sounds of a foreign language spoken throughout my home only made me feel more disconnected and alone. The smell of a warm cracked can of Budweiser beer permeated the walls within our home. I could take a whiff of air and thought it smelled similar to someone's vomit. A bottle of vodka, a plate of sliced ham with tomato and onions loaded with cracked pepper and salt on top were often left on the kitchen table after a party, which was almost every weekend.

My father would rock me every now and then in his brown wooden rocking chair, and it was somewhat felt comforting for me at times. The gentle rock made me feel as if everything was going to be okay. I could finally fall asleep to the gentle rock and rest my head on my dad's big shoulders and bare chest.

I shared a bedroom with my middle sister, Lina, on the first floor directly across my mom and dad's bedroom. Lina and I had shared twin bunk beds, and I preferred to normally sleep on the bottom bunk. Lina and I sometimes slept together in the same bunk, curled up, because we felt a little safer together during some nights. There was constant noise throughout the home and often rage followed. Sometimes a loud TV or maybe the music turned up a little too high. Often, there was noise from Mom's company of friends or family, which ultimately turned into loud arguments after too much vodka.

On one particular evening, we couldn't fall asleep because we could hear heavy stomping throughout the house. My father started to pace around the house and slam the doors. Lina and I were too scared to leave our room. A loud rage was heard from the living room.

"I WILL KIIILL YOU, Jana!" my father shouted from across the first-level home with a Slavic accent. "YOU FUCKING WHORE!"

I walked out of our bedroom to peek into the living room. I found my dad dressed in a white ribbed tank, oversized Hanes underwear, and bare-foot, standing in front of my mom while she was cornered in our living room wall far from the door, where she couldn't get away. My dad had one of his legs pushed forward while the other was bent behind him in front of my mom. I could spot an open can of beer next to the wooden rocker.

I saw my dad standing in front of Mom against the wall in a chokehold, with a pocket knife held against the side of her throat. My dad mumbled under his breath while white foam filled the corners of his mouth which ran down the side of his mouth and asked sadly, "Where were you, Jana? I waited all night for you to come home."

My dad's voice quickly turned as he shouted, "Were you fucking around, Jana? Who were you fucking around with? I know you were out because I followed you!" My dad slowly slid the knife across the right side of her neck just enough to break skin until she shed a few drops of blood.

My mom cried out, "I was working, and you are drunk again with the girls home. Don't do this, Alec! Why were you drinking again, Alec?"

As my mom moved an inch away, she screamed out in worry, "Where are the girls, Alec? You look like a disgusting animal raging in this home. Why don't you just get the fuck off of me and out of my life once and for all. I need to check on the girls!"

Dad said, "No, Jana! Not until you tell me where you were!"

Mom whimpered, "I told you I was working late, can't you see my cuts on my arm? Look at my hands, Alec! I am bruised from the assembly line at work. The line didn't stop tonight, and we had to work overtime!"

Then a moment later, my dad took a glance at her arms and slowly put his hand down next to the side of his body, with the knife slightly smeared with blood dangling in his hand. My mom ran into my arms and grabbed Lina and me close to her heart while sobbing with tears down her face.

My mom locked the front door of our bedroom and grabbed her keys and handbag. On the other side of our bedroom was a back door that led to the front porch with the main exit door of the home. Lina, Mom, and I quietly snuck out the front door and left for Grandma Baba's house. It was 2:00 a.m. and my mom was so exhausted from the lack of sleep and late hours at work she could barely stay awake behind the wheel. I could see my mom's eyelids flutter while she drove us to my grandma's house down the dark and empty roads.

My grandma lived about fifteen minutes away with both aunts and my older sister's family in a two-family home. My two aunts lived upstairs with my grandma, and my older sister lived downstairs with her family. My grandma Baba was widowed from my grandpa Jaja for many years now. Baba came to the US with Jaja in hopes of a better life, but she was faced with too many obstacles post World War II. Baba's birthplace was Ukraine, but she was later transported to Germany during World War II as a young girl at age fifteen or sixteen years old. It was mandatory for one family member to be taken out of the household to work in the camps during wartime. Baba worked for the Germans at a working camp in Germany where she soon met Jaja. Jaja was born in Latvia, but he was also that one family member transported to Germany to work at a camp where he met our beautiful Baba. Soon after, my grandparents gave birth to their firstborn daughter, my mom, and named her Jana. My grandparents had their second child also, my uncle, about two years later. After that, my grandparents moved their family back to Latvia, where my grandfather was raised. After the family moved back to Latvia, my mom and uncle were soon blessed with my grandparents' third child, my beautiful aunt Kazia. My mom said Latvia was so beautiful and she really enjoyed living there. My mom often reminded us how clean the country of Latvia was kept and she loved walking into the village. My mom often told us stories of how she kept busy ice skating in cold weather, and she had many friends around town and at school. My mom said they grew up on a family farm with fresh eggs, milk, and chickens, but the farm was eventually taken away. Work was scarce and so were the family meals. Mom told us she had to eat every piece of bread crumb on her plate before she was excused from the dinner table or her father, Jaja, became very, very upset.

Life became harder post war, and the family farm was taken away, and so was their source of income. Jaja wanted a better life for his family so they planned their trip to America, the land of opportunity and freedom. My mom said she cried when she heard the news, and she begged my grandma to let her stay in Latvia. My grandma found my mom was not old enough at the age of fifteen to stay in Latvia without her parents, so she was forced to move. My mom said she became very sad to learn she had to leave her friends and school behind for a new home in a totally different country at age sixteen.

Mom said she still remembers the day they flew into the US airport. It was a long flight to the USA, and she wondered why the airport wasn't as clean as the country of Latvia. Mom said her family couldn't understand English nor speak the language, and it was tough for Jaja to make his way around. A family member directed Baba and Jaja to the Manhattan area for work, and the family eventually found housing in Harrison, New Jersey. Work was not as easy to find in America, and it soon became disappointing for Jaja. Baba just gave birth to her fourth child, Tessa, so she could not contribute to the bills.

After a few years passed, Jaja passed away, and Baba was left to raise her family alone with no life insurance and very little money to survive. My uncle moved out of Grandma Baba's home to marry and raise a family. My aunt Kazia was still living at home and working to pay most of the house bills. Tessa was the youngest sibling and still in school. Baba loved children, animals, God, and songwriter Neil Diamond. Baba often chose a house dress over pants and she always wore a *hooska* to cover her hair all day and even at night to bed. Baba had primarily spoken Latvian in the home, but she understood very little English. I wondered why Baba often double-locked the doors behind her and kept to herself. It was later assumed that our Baba had bad experiences in the working camp and since then, had little trust for strangers. When we needed a place to stay, Baba would open her door and home for us to stay. When my mom ran away from my dad, Baba let us in for the night, but she often felt that my mom should soon return to her husband, Alec, to work out their unresolved issues. Baba believed Mom and Dad had to work harder at their problems and even ask God to help with prayer because she felt we all belonged back home as a family together.

My father would make an appearance every now and then at Baba's house on the hunt for my mom. We would all hide under the blankets in fear when we hear his loud stomping up the huge flight of stairs. You could hear my father near from miles away because he had such a powerful presence. When my father would knock on the door, Baba would answer and say, "Hello, Alec."

My father would say, "Hello, Baba," followed by his first question, "Where is Jana?"

Baba would say, "She is working, Alec, and not here."

Dad would then ask where the kids were. Baba would say, "Sleeping, Alec! Be good, Alec. No drink and go home to sleep!"

We would all be relieved when we heard Baba double-lock the front door shut. Baba had a way of calming my dad's rage and protecting Lina and me from our fear.

Bang! Bang! My mom knocked on Baba's door at almost 2:30 a.m. and cried, "Please let us in. Alec is drunk again, and the girls and I are scared Alec will kill us. Alec had a knife against my throat, and we cannot sleep. Alec tried to kill me! Please let us in!"

Baba said, "Okay, okay, come in." Baba would allow Lina and me to sleep in her bed with her, but my mom had to sleep on the sofa. My aunt Kazia slept in one bedroom, and my aunt Tessa in the other. Since it was only a two-bedroom apartment, my grandma made a bedroom out of the front porch. Babcha's room was filled with religious pictures and spiritual chachkas. I recall my grandma's bedroom was small, but her bed was piled high with the most comfortable feather bedding ever; she would pile on layers. Lina and I enjoyed our stay at Babcha's house. Our aunts were a lot of fun, and Baba was so kind, with a caring and beautiful soul. Baba's house became our safe house. There was always canned food in her cupboard and a big pot of compote with a variety of berries boiling on the stove to first cool and then drink. Lina and I would sink into her bedding and fall fast asleep when Baba sang us this Polish lullaby that sounded like this:

Aaa, kotki dwa,
szarobure obydwa,

nic nie będą robiły,
tylko ciebie bawiły.

It translated to a song sung about how no one can get you and you are safe in my arms.

SMAAASH! I woke up from a light sleep. It wasn't even two hours later until we heard my mom's car's glass windows shatter. There was no warning sign, knock, or yell, but we knew my dad was back! I peeked outside the window to find my father with a metal hammer in his hand smashing all five windows of my mom's silver Monte Carlo, one by one.

"You bitch! I will find you and kill you, Jana! Did you think you could hide? I will get you and kill you!" You could hear my dad in a severe rage from inside Baba's porch. My father found us! Oh no, he wanted to take revenge on my mom for leaving the house without him knowing. I could hear the glass shatter all over the street from my grandma's bedroom front porch.

"Where is she? Where is Jana?" yelled my father. "You better let me in or I will fucking kill you!"

I wanted to stay snug and safe in my grandma's bed until it all was over. I didn't want to open my eyes until my dad was gone.

My grandma made sure her front door was double-bolted with a chain lock. No one called the police because they were probably too fearful my dad would find out. Dad was about six feet two inches, 270, with strength I still can't quite comprehend. Baba hugged Lina and me tight until all the noise stopped and my dad disappeared. All I could think of was how loud the noise was of the glass shattering against the ground outside. My poor grandma was faced with such extreme embarrassment from my father's violent and obnoxious behavior. What did Baba's neighbors think of my family? We were so close to the family next door, but I thought it was possible that our friends' parents no longer wanted to allow us to play together. At least until the violent behavior died down.

We drove back home the next day in mom's car with busted glass in all four windows. My dad reappeared at our home a few days later to apologize, with tears flowing down his face. I started to notice Dad made a habit out of these appearances after he would act in a super violent manner, and it was all so disappointing. I could hear Dad at the front door whimpering in sorrow.

"Jana, please let me in. I am so sorry for my words and what I did to you. I love you, and I want to see the girls. Please, where are Lina and Tania? I want to see my children. We are a family. Please! Please! I want to see Lina and Tania?"

I peeked over the living room wall to find my dad begging my mom, attempting to kiss her and make up. My dad immediately shouted, "Tania, my baby!"

My father picked me up way high to the sky, twirled me around, and whispered in his Slavic accent, "My baby girl. I love you, and I missed you so much!" It was a feeling of protection I had missed and longed for with a passion from my dad.

We couldn't understand why dad behaved this way when his entire family was responsible and non-violent. We were told Dad was never the same since he saw his dad shot by a German soldier. Mom often forgave dad and let him back in the home until the next time—and there always seemed to be a never-ending next time.

It was 8:00 a.m., and Lina missed another day at school. I couldn't remember learning much in school except for during my elementary years when I won spelling bees and received A-plus grades in math! I really enjoyed spelling bee competitions, but I longed to see my mom or dad in the crowd when I glanced down while I was on stage. I would quickly lose concentration on stage and thoughts of my mom raced past my mind. I was worried for my mom and prayed she was alive and okay. I didn't see my mom often, but I still knew I needed her, and I wanted to see her more. I often remembered when I anticipated and hoped that I would look up in the audience just once to find my mom's beautiful face at my spelling bee event. What a surprise it would have been to see my mom smile, but she was nowhere to be found. I wanted my mom and dad to be proud of me and see how well I could spell and even WIN first place, but I was often disappointed to look up and find many unfamiliar faces in the crowd. My mom and dad missed another school event.

Still, I enjoyed my elementary days of Catholic school at times, and I felt a sense of peace there. During those moments when I lost concentration in class or felt extreme worry, I would look up and find Jesus Christ hung up on the cross, and it settled my stomach for a few minutes. Hail Mary and Our Father prayers were often recited in the beginning or at the end of class, and we were let out early on Friday to attend mass at noon. I enjoyed spending time with my friends when I was actually able to make it into class, but it wasn't regular. Lina and I had many absences from all the noise and chaos we grew up in and the lack of sleep we had. Our principal and teachers knew the circumstances and kept my family close in their prayers. Memories of elementary school became a blur, and I recall only wanting to be around my sister Lina since my mom wasn't around often. Friends would invite me over to their home, but I was afraid to leave my sister Lina. I wanted to follow her everywhere, but she didn't always want her baby sister around. I felt like a tagalong at times, but being with Lina was most comforting for me. Lina asked why I didn't want to spend time with my friend Heather when she asked me to come over to her home after school. I couldn't quite explain why I felt the way I did, but I knew that I didn't want to go over Heather's home. I was too sad, scared, worried, and upset, but I couldn't quite find the words to say it. I wasn't in touch with my emotional side at age seven, so I held my worries in as most children do.

I didn't have a large appetite as a child, but I did enjoy my pizza the most when I ate. I also enjoyed our school lunches which consisted of a different menu every day. The hamburger sloppy joes served on a soft bun were always so tasty, but the hamburger patties were plain in taste and mostly dry. Sometimes, I would skip my lunch if I didn't have enough money or Mom forgot to pay ahead. I would starve at times, and my tummy would growl in class, but I was too embarrassed to ask anyone to borrow money. I couldn't wait to get home on those days I skipped lunch. Sometimes Lina and I could scrounge up enough change to stop at Dairy Queen for a homemade iced tea or hot pretzel to hold us off until we got home. By the time, Lina and I walked home, we were so hungry we would open up a can of whatever we could find in the lazy Susan to eat. Often, we could find a can of SpaghettiOs, and if we were really lucky, we could open up a box of pizza rolls found in the freezer. Our last resort was a can of corn to take us through the night. Most of our elementary and middle school days were lonely. No one was home when we arrived after school since Mom had to work the third shift and Dad wasn't around.

Chapter 2

Only the Lonely

Years passed filled with heartache, pain, confusion, and sadness. I never had a chance to get to know my father's family too well, and most days seemed to be a fog. I was only eight years old when my dad finally passed away. I remember hearing my mom scream on the phone when she received the news.

"Lina! Tania!" shouted my mom. "Your father is dead! Oh my gosh! I can't believe Alec is dead!"

It was so horrifying to hear my dad passed away, but it was also a bit of a relief that it wasn't my mom who passed first. My dad passed away in his sleep at a friend's house in the middle of the night, the day after his birthday on a cold February morning. Dad and Mom were not getting along very well, but they were not officially divorced. Dad often stayed at a friend's house when he drank too much, and he and Mom fought often, so they were finally estranged. More bad news hit our family's home, and it was official. Dad's body was examined twice, and he was pronounced dead. I can still recall the smell of the potent incense in the Orthodox Church on the day of my father's funeral. The Orthodox mass was in an uptight and impersonal style, unlike any other funeral I saw on TV. I couldn't believe my father's body was laid out and open to view only a few steps away from us! It was too close of an encounter for a little girl to witness, but I hung in there. It was my first funeral, and I wanted to be there to understand the story.

We all were given cream-colored candles that were already lit to hold while we walked around my father's casket and kissed him goodbye. The Orthodox priest shook his thurible or censer and chanted words in a language I couldn't understand. Tears shed on many faces that day, and the sound of a crowd crying was heard throughout. My mother grabbed my oldest sister, Julia, tight in her arms to hug her before she fainted on the tiled and cold ground next to my father in the middle of mass!

Following the mass was the wake, and I wanted to be present once again, but Lina did not. I can recall walking into the funeral home to hear my grandma screaming in tears, "My Alec. No! My Alec! They killed him!"

My grandma shouted, "You killed him! YOU KILLED MY SON!" directly at my mom in front of the entire crowd.

My mom was so hurt, and her eyes were filled with tears. I was sad for Mom and so embarrassed for her because she really wouldn't hurt a fly. It was a major turning point in my life, and there was a void I longed to be filled for many, many years ahead. It was also the last time I spent time with my dad's mom (Grandma) for about fifteen years. Still, I yearned for a father-and-daughter bond, which was taken from me too soon.

Although we mourned the loss of my dad, we were able to get some peace and quiet in our home, and the worry of my father killing my mother subsided as time passed. Still, I missed my dad and thought about him often, especially on his birthday and the evening he died on the day before his birthday years later. I missed my dad when he was alive and healthy, and I missed him now that he was gone, but I had to face my father was finally gone from this Earth. I wondered why my dad behaved this way when he was alive, and I wondered why he treated my mom so badly. I wondered why my dad was the only adult in his family who behaved this way, and why he and Mom were not able to work out their issues. I wondered why my dad had died and left us all so soon. I felt sad and even more lonely and lost than ever. We had no patriarch of the family to provide, guide, or support our family. We didn't have the guidance, as children, when my father was alive or the love young children need. We were often faced with fits of rage, alcoholism, and abuse in early childhood and my siblings' teenage years.

Time passed, and I felt glad for my mom to be relieved of the physical, emotional, and verbal abuse. I was glad my mom was alive. I felt relieved to at least have two caring aunts and our loving Babcha with a huge heart on my mom's side of the family. My dad's side of the family distanced themselves from us because they blamed my mom for my dad's death. I am sure this resulted from one side of the story. My mom allowed several of her Latvian cousins to stay with us in our home while visiting when they visited America. In turn, Mom expected them to help care for Lina and me free of charge.

Mom had to support our family, and times were tough for her even though my older sister and brother were living out of the home. My brother left the home at an early age so he could escape the chaos and violence in our home. I couldn't imagine being in my brother's circumstance—to arrive home only to find your dad locked you out of your own home one fine day after school, for no apparent reason. Sadly, it was well-known in the local community that my dad also tried to kill my brother for protecting my mom.

Even though it was just Lina and me left inside the home, Mom had to make ends meet. Mom decided that it was best to rent out the upstairs apartment to a family member so there was an adult in the home after my dad passed. Still, Lina and I were on our own for dinner and on our own with extracurricular events or functions. Often, we didn't have a ride to any extracurricular activities so it was rare that we completed any program we enrolled in. Mom didn't normally arrive home until 3:00 a.m. from the late shift on the assembly line, and we were normally asleep by then. Unfortunately, Mom had to wake up a few hours later to drive Lina and me to school on only a few hours of sleep. We would try to leave early enough so we can stop at the bakery to pick up a Portuguese buttered roll or custard cup for breakfast. Mom was so tired driving us to school so she barely spoke any words. Our only time with Mom during the week was in the morning since Mom was gone by the time we arrived home from school.

Thankfully, we found some light when time was spent with a close childhood friend named Demi and her family. Sometimes our good friend Demi would spend the night over, and we were so thankful she would keep us company, especially on this one particular day. Demi, Lina, and I had just come back to our home from a bike ride around the neighborhood. We entered the kitchen to grab a bite when all of a sudden, the radio just blasted on its own. Demi and I looked up at the stereo system and found the picture also fell under the shelf near the stereo. What was happening? It was almost as if someone actually turned up our living room stereo's volume to full blast and then back down again. We never touched the stereo, so then who did? We then heard another noise coming from the front porch as if someone picked up a window shade and slammed it against the window. All three of us stopped whatever we were doing and ran into the bathroom, locked the door behind us, and hid in the tub for a few minutes until the noise was gone.

Demi ran out to the kitchen phone to call her dad and asked him to come by our home because of the noise we ALL heard. We knew something just wasn't right. Demi's dad came over within a few minutes, and he walked around the entire home to check for any opened windows. Demi's dad even checked the unfinished basement level of the home. Demi's dad closely inspected every window and door in the home but nothing seemed to be tampered with.

Later that evening, Demi's dad did mention seeing a strange vehicle with two men in what appeared to be gas man uniforms. The men were standing outside their vehicle a few homes away from our home, and it must have just dawned on him. Ironically, those same two men rang our bell earlier in the day and said they were the gas man when we shouted, "Who is it?" before leaving home for a walk. The two men must have observed our home for several hours now. Thankfully, Demi's dad thought it was just best that we all left the home for the night and stay over at Demi's home. We didn't feel safe at home, so we all took off for a night out at Demi's home. We figured our mom would realize we spent the night at Demi's home when she arrived that night.

That evening, my mom walked into a home completely ransacked. The door was left slightly open, and the lights were left on. Mom knew something wasn't right, and she said her stomach sank. Mom cried and prayed Lina and I were okay because she could not find us sleeping in our bedroom. The blankets were rolled up in the middle of the bed and her little girls were gone! The living room television and stereo were gone. Pictures were taken off the wall and blankets were thrown all over. Frozen meat was torn out of the freezer and left in the middle of the living room.

My mom immediately ran out of the home and called the local police. Mom then called Demi's mom, praying she would hear her girls were okay. We had minimal contact with Mom while she was at work so we didn't bother to inform her we planned to spend the night over Demi's home. Demi's mom woke us up the following morning to tell us she just hung up the phone with our mom and she was on her way over. Demi's mom said, "My sweet girls, sorry to inform you that your home was robbed, but your mom is okay."

We ALL thanked God again! Mom picked us up from Demi's home the next morning at about 7:00 a.m. How scary! OMG! Could my dad have tried to warn us to get out of the home? We often wondered if it was my dad who turned up that stereo volume. My dad was always the protective kind, and who knows if his spirit still lingered. I was later led to believe his spirit sure did for quite some time.

On another occasion, I thought I actually saw his translucent spirit appear. It was about 2:00 a.m. when my oldest sister, Julia, heard loud footsteps stomping up the staircase. Julia happened to stay over that night along with her daughter after a late family gathering. My sister Julia and her daughter slept in one of the twin beds while Lina, Colleen, our neighbor, and I slept on the floor. My aunt or Mom's cousin was visiting from Latvia, and she stayed in my bedroom. We all happened to be in the upstairs apartment when we heard the noise. *THUMP, THUMP, THUMP!* The sound of someone with heavy feet or work boots walking up the stairs was heard.

"Who's there?" yelled Julia. "Who is it? Someone look!"

Julia continued to shout, "Please, someone look!"

Julia screamed even louder in question, "Who is walking up the stairs?"

Since no one else responded, I was brave enough to pick my head up from my pillow to find what appeared to be a translucent image of my father dressed in the same gray-colored suit as he was dressed in on his funeral day. The sound of the footprints was his heavy boots! I could see this figure of what appeared to be my dad just watching over us with one arm raised against the wall.

I screamed, "Аннн!" and threw the covers back over my head.

My aunt ran over to our room from the other room and also swore she saw an image. Julia called 911 and screamed, "I think someone broke into our home!"

When the police arrived, they checked the entire home. Every window and door was checked to see if any were tampered with, but there was no evidence of break-in and entry. The police saw the bottle of vodka on the table and smirked.

"We're sorry, ma'am! There is no sign of entry here," said the officer. "There is no sign of a break and entry or any intruder entering the home. Are you sure you are okay? Have you been drinking too much?"

Julia thanked the officer, and we finally got some rest a few hours later.

A wise woman once later told me my father wasn't quite ready to leave his family behind, and his spirit was always around us. Mitzi was a predictor, but she could read some of the past. Mitzi was known to be one of Highland Park's finest predictors, and she was no witch! Mitzi came highly recommended by a friend of the family, but she was extremely blunt, no-nonsense, with minimal time on her hands.

When my aunt made the appointment to get her reading, Mitzi picked up the phone and said, "Hello? Who is this and what do you want?"

My aunt Kazia said, "You were recommended to us. My sister Janna and I would like to make an appointment."

Mitzi said, "Well, when do you want to come in? I don't have a lot of time, but let me check my book. Okay, I will see you and your sister tomorrow, but that's it. I can't do any more readings so don't expect anyone else to be given a reading."

After my mom hung up the phone, my aunt said aloud, "What an unpleasant witch!"

My aunt and mom traveled together to get the reading, but they felt a little uneasy and unwelcome.

Mitzi opened the door and said, "Do you have an appointment? What is your name?" My mom responded yes and announced their names as Jana and Kazia.

Mitzi said, "Okay, come in."

My mom said before she and Kazia could even sit down, they were greeted by the following: "I am Mitzi, and I have been helping people discover and predict their future for many, many years. I have worked with several government agencies on criminal and missing person cases and never advertised. Oh, and by the way... I am no witch!"

My aunt said her face dropped. My aunt Kazia could not believe she actually knew how my aunt felt about her! After my aunt told us the story, I thought this was someone I should definitely take the time out to visit. Shortly after, I made an appointment along with a friend and my sister Lina. Mitzi offered the same approach when we arrived and said, "Okay, who wants a reading first?"

I was always the brave one and offered to go first.

Mitzi sat me down to explain she was a predictor and focused her readings on the future. Mitzi asked me if it was okay to communicate everything she picked up from my energy even if it was offensive. Mitzi also asked me to promise her not to live in fear or according to her reading. Mitzi said I would need to live my life as normal following this reading and not worry about the future or the prediction

Mitzi would share. I agreed to Mitzi's terms, so she began her reading with a deck of picture cards.

Mitzi asked, "Who is this strong and protective man around you?" Mitzi stated firmly, "I feel a strong presence and energy around you."

I wasn't exactly sure what she was referring to at that second.

Mitzi said, "Did someone die recently you were very close to?"

My response was, "Oh, yes. My dad passed away, but it was a few years ago."

Mitzi said, "Yes, his spirit is always with you, watching over you girls." Mitzi continued, "He loved you all very much and didn't want to leave you all so soon, and he looks out for you often so his spirit is always with you."

I felt amazed that Mitzi picked up my dad's energy, and it was almost a supernatural feeling. I felt chills enter through my entire body in a wave-like form, and I knew there was some truth to that statement.

Mitzi said, "Your dad is here right now," as she looked up to the ceiling.

I smiled with a sense of relief and protection from my dad. My dad was actually with us, and I felt it! I knew I felt his energy around me, and I wasn't going crazy.

Mitzi proceeded with her reading and said she saw my hand in marriage more than once, but only two actual marriage commitments. I didn't quite understand her statement at that time, but I was intrigued by her words.

Mitzi said, "The first man will love you very much, and I don't want you to ever question that, but the second man will love you even more in the right way."

I wanted to hear more details, but there weren't many more to share. I had to wait for my future and live it as if I never received a reading from Mitzi. It wasn't so easy to follow Mitzi's terms, but I tried my best as she wished.

A few years later, my mom found her love and second husband at work. I was about thirteen years old when I first met my stepdad and about fourteen or fifteen when they decided to marry. My stepdad was so kind and extremely helpful, but it took some time to get familiar with each other. My stepdad was not quite as broad as my dad, but rather tall and lean. Our first bonding moment was when I woke up and heard my stepdad play a birthday song over the speaker on my sixteenth birthday.

It was a sunny morning, and I was happy to share my birthday with my new stepdad. I watched my stepdad sing along to the whole verse as he grabbed my hand to dance around.

Sixteen Candles by the Crests

Happy birthday, happy birthday,
   baby
Oh, I love you so

Sixteen candles make a lovely
light
But not as bright as your eyes
tonight
Blow out the candles
Make your wish come true
For I'll be wishing that you love
me too
You're only sixteen but you're my
teenage queen
You're the prettiest, loveliest girl
I've ever seen
Sixteen candles in my heart will
glow
Forever and ever for I love you so
You're only sixteen but you're my
teenage queen
You're the prettiest, loveliest girl
I've ever seen
Sixteen candles in my heart will
glow
Forever and ever for I love you so
You're only sixteen, but you're my
teenage queen
Oh, you're the prettiest
Loveliest girl I've ever seen

Sixteen candles in my heart will
glow
For ever and ever for I love you so
For I love you so

My stepdad was a true blessing to our family, and we quickly became grateful for him appearing at such a difficult time for all of us. Although my father could never be replaced, my stepdad filled a piece of that void through the immense love and care he shared for my siblings and me.

As the years passed, we grew closer and developed a stronger bond of trust with a higher level of love. My stepdad was always there for us with patience, open arms, and a helping hand. I couldn't believe how hard of a worker my stepdad was and all the selfless time he devoted to helping my family around us. My stepdad became crowned as the family's savior!

Time healed us because we were all scarred by the loss of my dad, in one form or another. Time passed and even healed some of the family's pain. We finally were able to rest at night and redirect our focus in life. I became attracted to something of a similar resemblance to my biological dad and even married someone several years older at such a young age. Still, I mourned the loss of my biological dad when most didn't know it. It was like a huge empty gap within me, and I felt so sad and alone too often. I wished my dad was healthier and alive. It was my first attachment to love that was taken away too soon.

Chapter 3

Obsession

When I met my husband, I was totally taken by a force I felt I could not control. I was asked out to dinner as a favor for my close childhood girlfriend, Demi. Demi and I stayed close friends throughout our entire childhood and I never forgot how great her family was to Lina and so I would do anything for her! I wasn't exactly sold on the guy of interest during that time, and I really had no intentions of meeting my soon-to-be husband or father to my child. My girlfriend Demi called me several times to please do her this favor, and it was only going to be a dinner for a few hours at a beautiful restaurant with an awesome view of the New York skyline. I was only nineteen years old and not many of my friends had this opportunity. I was extremely mature and interested in the total experience so I caved in and agreed. I thought we were all together, so what could possibly go wrong?

I wore a beautiful two-piece dark brown fitted pantsuit with a fur collar and high heels. I had long, bright blond hair and a nice shape. I wasn't too thin, but I was far from chubby. I finally started to enjoy life and the smile on my face probably gave that away! It wasn't long before I was picked up in a brand new Cadillac sedan and treated to a top-notch dinner and drinks all picked up by this generous businessman, Joseph. My girlfriend's cousin was looking to find work for Joseph, and so the deal was sealed. I remember my bestie Demi walking closely with Joseph in the parking lot together, and I thought for sure Joseph was interested in Demi, and I couldn't wait for Demi to fill me in on their private conversation. It was totally clear that Demi believed in romantic love more than I did at that time. I was totally thrown off when Demi asked me what I thought of Joseph.

I said, "Me? What do you mean, Demi? I thought Joseph was totally into you, and I thought for sure you might hit it off."

Demi responded with a clear and firm "No. He asked about you! He asked for your phone number so you could go out sometime on his boat."

I was shocked and at a loss for words! I truly thought Joseph and Demi were totally flirting and had some connection together.

It was only about two days later when my phone rang, and sure enough, it was Joe asking when I would go for a cruise on his thirty-eight-foot Cigarette racing boat. I had never been on a boat that size nor have I ever been on a speedboat! This was all very exciting, but I wasn't quite ready to be alone with Joe, so we held off for a bit. Demi had planned a movie night over the weekend with a few friends and asked if I would join them. Demi mentioned that Joe would be there, and it might be a chance for me to get to know him a bit more. I didn't think it would hurt me none since it was another group outing so I agreed to join. Besides, the movie choice was my kind titled *Armageddon*, starring Liv Tyler, Ben Affleck, and Bruce Willis.

Joe became more persistent and rang my phone again the next day. Joe asked when I would take a ride down on his boat. Once again, I was flattered and it felt exciting, but I didn't know Joe very well and he was older than most of the boys I was friends with. I told Joe that I would go for a ride on his boat under one condition and that would be if a friend came along. Although I had an attraction for older men, I was still somewhat intimidated by them. Joe and I agreed on a plan, and I brought along a friend on our boat ride. The boat was fast, but the company was fun. We ordered dinner in, and my friend and I drove back home.

It was only a week later before I received my first rose delivery at work. The roses were so large, sparkly, and beautiful! I have never received a bouquet of flowers let alone one that beautiful and expensive! I thought for sure this charming guy was interested in me, and I thought about how lucky I was. The deliveries became regular, and I received a different color fresh bouquet of full-stemmed roses with baby's breath every week sent to my office! My office was soon surrounded by so many beautiful roses they no longer fit by my desk. I had to begin transport the roses to my car for home. Even if I placed the bouquet of roses on the floor, water still found its way to seep all over my rug in my car. I had to eventually grow up and face Joe alone on a date, so I agreed to Joe's request. My next date was solo with Joe at an Italian restaurant. We had a great conversation, and the food was top notch. I loved how special Joe made me feel and how he treated me like a lady, unlike I have ever been treated before. Chivalry was not dead.

Some time had passed, and Joe and I grew closer, and we started speaking a few times a day. I started to gain Joe's trust more every day but especially one particular evening over a serious conversation. Joe drove over to my mom's house to tell me that he had a son who lived in Florida with his mom and grandparents. Joe said it was a one-night stand, and there was never a relationship with his child's mom, but he financially supports him. Joe said he didn't see him much because of the distance, and it was probably better that way under their circumstance. Joe didn't want to confuse the child, and he made it very clear that his son would never affect our lives. I thought the situation was odd, but I understood that the distance between them may have been a barrier. I wasn't exactly sure what he meant by that, and I asked what would happen if his son wanted to learn more about his dad later in life and came out to find him. Joe seemed very bothered by that question, and he asked me to drop the conversation and not to mention it ever again. I thought it was an emotional subject, and I could tell it bothered Joe. Since it was a touchy subject, I thought it was best to respect Joe's wishes and not discuss it further, so I never brought it up again for a very long while. I honored that Joe was upfront and honest with me.

Joe seemed to want to spend more and more time together, and he soon asked that I drive his extra car since it was safer than my Nissan. I never asked or thought of driving a Cadillac, but I thought I would go with it since Joe insisted it was an extra car and it was a lot larger than mine. The Cadillac was not a car I would ever choose to buy or drive, but Joe said he wanted me to drive it and it would make him happy if I did. I didn't have to pay for gas or maintenance. I felt so flattered and thought it would be okay to drive every now and then, until one very sad and disappointing and evening.

I drove down to see Joe in his green Cadillac. The plan was to hang out in the Jacuzzi and possibly go out on his jet ski or boat, but I just so happened to be only five minutes later than expected. Joe was calling me in the car, but I could not answer the phone because I was driving. I couldn't see as well in the dark, and I wasn't exactly on-point, driving someone else's car. I felt like I had to pay more attention to the road and take extra caution. When I arrived at Joe's house, I knocked at the door and then opened the screen door to knock. Joe opened the door in a very rough manner and actually pushed me so hard away from his entryway that I was flung down the two stairs and onto his rocks. I was SHOCKED! Could this really be happening?

Joe yelled out, "You are late, Tania! I tried to call you a few times, but you didn't answer."

I didn't answer the phone because I was busy driving making my way down to Joe's house. I was concerned for my safety over punctuality. I picked myself up while tears began to run down my cheek. I didn't say much more, and I just got back in the car and drove all the way back home. For the first time, I felt pain deep within from someone other than my dad, and my heart shattered from the pain I felt. I felt it was just wiser not to say much since I had to get home, and I wasn't sure what would transpire if I stayed at Joe's place much longer.

I couldn't believe someone could turn on me that quickly. Joe was not right, and I wasn't going to bother with him any longer. I didn't answer his calls on my way home while driving his car, but I knew he would be around soon to pick up his vehicle. I also told my mom the story and asked her not to let him around me as I didn't want to see him anymore. What became even more upsetting was that my mom didn't believe me, and she sided with Joe on his story. Joe immediately called my mom and manipulated the story. Joe told her that I aggressively pushed my way in the door, which I would have no reason to do so. I couldn't believe my mom actually believe him and even sided with Joe. My mom asked me if I was all right and that she hoped I would behave nicely. I told my mom that I would leave Joe's keys in the kitchen drawer for him to pick up. I felt so crushed so I ran upstairs to my room and shut out the household. I cried myself to tears that night. I finally became close to someone I was truly intrigued by, and he hurt me! Although I was so confused, I knew the behavior was not right, so I ignored all of Joe's calls that evening and told my mom I wanted no part of him EVER AGAIN or his phone or car for that matter!

The following day, Joe appeared at my mom's house, begging me to forgive him and said he promised that would never happen again. Joe apologized to my mom and said he wanted me to have his extra phone at no cost to me. I really didn't want his phone, but he insisted and said it was free of charge. Joe said he was going to leave it behind whether I wanted it or not because he had several lines included in his cell package. I thought that was very generous, but I was still upset.

Joe teared up as he walked away to speak to my mom in the kitchen. Joe told my mom that he loved me and that he was so sorry about the other night. A few hours later, my mom finally started to see there was more to Joe's original story, and she apologized to me. Mom thought it might be okay to give it another try, but she told me to be very careful. I was grateful my mom finally believed that I wasn't in the wrong. Why would anyone make up a story like that? I realized my mom was totally naive and more gullible than I ever thought, but she was still my mom, and

I needed her support because she still was the closest person to me.

I was unsure of Joe and had mixed feelings. How could someone truly care for me and hurt me that way? The next time, Joe appeared at my mom's home was with a gift box in his hand. Joe said he picked it up for me the other day just because. I opened the box with a Bloomingdale's necklace pouch to find a beautiful gold-and-silver necklace. I couldn't believe this was a gift picked up for me! It looked high-quality and a shiny piece of art that was not very cheap. I absolutely loved it, and it put a smile on my face. I never owned any piece of jewelry that expensive, and I thought it was so tasteful. I began to admire Joe for his generosity and felt so appreciative. In the following week or so came the matching earrings as another gift! When I wore the set to dinner, it made me feel so special and gorgeous! I thought for sure Joe was serious about our relationship, and for sure, he was sorry. I felt like Joe was sure he wouldn't jeopardize what we had this time around. The next few weeks, Joe spent most of his time, energy, and focus on me; and things seemed to finally be looking upward.

Joe and I both shared an interest in real estate. We began to drive around different neighborhoods and check out different home styles and landscapes in the Westchester and Upstate New York area often. I always enjoyed the rides along the country roads while we listened to the radio. Since I had a thirst for knowledge, I was totally intrigued by anything and everything Joe said. Joe and I starting spending most of our time near the Long Island shore community, and it began to feel so comfortable as if I were exactly where I was supposed to be. Joe normally liked the driver's seat, but this time, he asked me to take the wheel so I drove the boat!

Joe and I were on his boat, and we just came back from a ride with Barry White blasted on the radio. Joe attacked me in his boat in a playful manner and told me he loved me that night and hoped that I loved him too. I did begin to fall for Joe, and I told him his feelings were reciprocated. There was a sense of comfort and security I longed to feel, and I finally filled that void in Joe's arms. It was only five months later when Joe told me he loved me so much that he wanted to spend the rest of his life together. Soon after, we went shopping for engagement rings.

I loved the two-carat round stone, but Joe pointed out an even larger stone he felt was more beautiful on my finger. After dinner one fine evening, Joe got down on one knee and opened up a green box with a 3.2-carat marquise-cut diamond ring. My jaw dropped, and my eyes sparkled from the diamond. That ring was meant to be on my finger, and it looked perfect on me! It was so beautiful that it made me feel like a princess! Everyone stopped to glance at my finger everywhere we went. I would catch couples staring at the ring from afar while we were dining. I was so young with such a gorgeous stone on my finger, and I wore it with pride every chance I could. On rare occasions, I left the stone home so I wouldn't feel uncomfortable around those less fortunate. I was very protective of my stone and made sure it was always kept in a safe place when not on my finger.

I began dress shopping for our wedding day in excitement. The woman at the bridal salon's eyes almost popped out when she saw my ring. She asked for my hand as a close-up and then commented that someone must love me very, very much! I responded with "Thank you, I guess he does," but still I wondered if Joe really did love me. Random women would ask to see my ring close up while in public, and my family was in awe. My sister Julia even asked to try it on. I was later told that it was bad luck to let anyone try on your ring. Could it be coincidental or just a silly superstition someone made up?

The wedding plans began, and we were seriously stressed out. We had placed a 50 percent down payment on the wedding hall, and I picked out wine-colored dresses for my bride's maids. I had five bridesmaids I asked to form my bridal party and all five accepted! I was so excited I didn't know where to direct my focus next. My mom thought the date picked for the wedding was too soon, but Joe pushed for that date and said he had it taken care of. My mom told us she would need a year to save for financials, but Joe didn't want any part of my parent's contributions and said he had a thriving business that brought in enough money. It was tough to argue against Boss Man, but Mom shared her one wish with me and that was to follow through with my college education no matter how much excess money we had or how successful the business was. It was just as important to my mom as it was to me, and I made her that promise I planned to keep.

Along with the wedding plans were the house plans to manage all at the same time! Everything moved so fast, but Joe wouldn't have it any other way! Joe was fast, aggressive, courageous, and he knew exactly what he wanted. Joe was no amateur, and he knew how to execute his plan at any expense. People could see Joe also had a charismatic and charming personality and could gain your attention in a split second. Joe had a way of getting others to become completely intrigued by his presence fairly quickly, and it was quite impressive, like none I have ever known. People reacted to Joe with all eyes when he walked into a room with his strong and power-ful presence. Maybe it was because Joe was fearless and everyone could sense that energy. Maybe it was because Joe was determined and everyone knew it to be true. Maybe it was because it was all of the above along with Joe's height and build and everyone could see it. His presence, voice, and motion made it clear who was boss; and he was soon to be my husband in a very exciting life! Joe was 100 percent sure of his decisions, and he would only have it his way. We also found a home we began new construction on in the midst of all the wedding planning. Joe wanted to live fairly close to the water, and I wanted to live near my family, so we eventually settled on midway just a few minutes south of my family and a few miles from an up-and-coming beach town. There was so much work to do, but it was all so exciting! I didn't want to brag about my new plans in life, so I remained humbled and left my ring behind one evening out with friends. That didn't pan out so well when Joe appeared at the tavern my friends decided to meet up in. Joe barged right into the patio area.

"What are you doing?" asked Joe. "I called you a few times, and you didn't answer."

I told Joe I was out with my friends and didn't get to my phone yet. I stepped away from my girl-friends at the tavern table to meet Joe outside since the conversation became loud. I honestly needed some time with my friends.

Joe screamed, "Where is your ring? You left your ring home?" I told Joe I did because I didn't want to be the center of attention or let anyone feel bad. I was the first person in my town's circle to get engaged, let alone with a 3.2-carat ring. I was very young with an older fiancé, and I wasn't excited about being questioned. Joe flipped in the middle of the patio bar and stormed out and off into his new Mercedes sedan where he drove off like a maniac! I was mortified by the number of people who witnessed, so I left the bar. I apologized over and over and finally let it go until the next incident that occurred. I realized all would work out fine as long as Joe had full control, but there was a problem as soon as I was out of his sight even for a minute. I was stressed out and unsure of how to manage this behavior.

On another occasion, I was shopping at Home Goods when Joe busted in my line to yell out, "I have been trying to contact you! What the hell are you doing?"

Once again, I was embarrassed and shocked that Joe would actually appear in the Home Goods store to find me shopping for a belt. I was so nervous that I dropped my purchase on the floor and then picked it up to place quickly place back on the conveyor belt. I looked up from my purchase and replied, "Buying a belt."

"What are you doing?" Joe blurted out. "I was so nervous! Someone could have stolen you?"

I questioned and replied, "Steal me? We are in Westchester, New York! No one is going to steal me, Joe!" We were in broad daylight inside the store! The cashier was at a loss for words.

That night, I made a decision to let Joe know this relationship just wasn't working out and something was off. I couldn't quite place my finger on it but something felt deeply wrong. I became stressed out, and I couldn't manage this demanding and aggressive and intrusive behavior. I gave Joe back his ring and said I just couldn't continue like this with the marriage plans. Joe apologized in tears and blamed his behavior on all the stress of the wedding and home. Joe said he was sorry if he came across as overbearing, but he only wanted to begin a life with me and that nothing else mattered.

Joe said, "I love you, Tania, and I don't care if we throw a wedding party or not. In fact, I don't need a party or a bachelor party. My whole life was a bachelor party. I want to start a life with you in our big home and fill it with a family of our own. I love you for all you are, and I will support you through your education. You may work if you want to work and not work if you do not want to, but I would love for you to work for us and build our own empire. I have big plans for us, Tania, and we are going to live a fabulous life without any worry and lots of money! You are going to be well taken care of and never want for anything. I can provide a better life for you than anyone else ever could. In turn, you will be the mother of our children, care for our son and support me with the family business. You don't even have to cook or clean because we can hire a service. Please, don't throw this away. I promise to give you the very best of the best and more than anyone else could provide. Also, we already started building our beautiful home, Tania. I love you, Tania, with all my heart!"

I looked into Joe's eyes, and he seemed so sincere. I caught a glimpse of a teardrop running down Joe's face. I loved him now more than ever, and I just couldn't give up and throw away what we already built.

We agreed to call off the wedding party and decided to elope to Hawaii. We had lost the 50 percent deposit on the banquet hall and also 25 percent on the bridal dress party, but there was no time to waste. We were going to elope to Hawaii in only one month away. I already purchased my dress, and we already had our bands. We called the banquet hall to arrange for flowers, a photographer, and a minister. We booked our flights and took off for the beautiful island of Hawaii at the Four Seasons Resort. The ceremony went fairly smoothly, and we had a lovely time away. Our time away finally felt like a break from all the planning and chaos, but it didn't seem long enough. My parents were the witnesses to our marriage, and we began married life together!

Our days flew by, and time seemed to be turned on to rush mode. Every day was like Christmas. Extra money was always at hand. I was smothered with lavish gifts of which included furs, jewels, and trendy clothing. It seemed as though I received a gift just because every other weekend, which consisted of a fur sweater or a gold bracelet just because. Every time we went out to shop, Joe was ready to make a purchase, so maybe that was how Joe expressed his love? Joe and I ate at the finest restaurants, and we enjoyed top entertainment such as New York Broadway shows and comedy clubs. Joe often treated my family to top restaurants and even picked them up with a limousine car service. Life was just grand and any pain that Joe may have caused seemed to subside. We had three to four vehicles at one time, which included luxury and sports vehicles. There never seemed enough time to just enjoy the present because life moved fast. Joe was so financially driven, and of course, had to be in charge.

Joe decided to sell his home near the beach so we can gain a fresh start in a new family community with a top-rated school system. Since Joe was in the process of selling his home, it was agreed upon that he live with myself and my parents until our home was fully constructed.

Within a few months, we were in our beautiful 4600-square-foot home! I had to pick out a paint color, tile, and flooring. I shopped for bedding, drapery, and furniture for our home, and it was all so exciting! I fell in love with a particular furniture store that sold contemporary furniture so we bought most of our furnishings from a dealer twenty miles north of our home. Our home was finally furnished with top-quality design furnishings and custom drapes in no time! Our cabinets were marble and all floors were hardwood. Our in-ground pool was surrounded by California stone. We had professional landscaping with beautiful lights that lit up our light-gray-colored colonial-style home at night. We had the best of the best, and it was all absolutely stunning. Joe said it was decorated like a museum, and everyone admired the home's decor in all white and black. We ordered beautiful artwork painted by a Russian artist to hang on our walls, and we had a top-of-the-line sound system. Our family and friends were so impressed with our work, and they absolutely loved it. In fact, my sister Lina loved it so much she moved in for a short week's stay. Lina didn't want to go home! Business was booming, and I was still focused and commuting to college class.

Only six months later, I was blessed with the news that we were going to have a baby! Joe wanted to immediately share the news with his mom, but I told him I was not ready just yet. I had to take it all in and accept that my life would soon change forever. I had a feeling the baby was a boy, but we confirmed at our earliest chance. Joe asked why I thought the baby was a boy, and I told him that I had a good feeling my dad's good energy would live on through this child. I also felt it was a chance for Joe to develop a beautiful relationship with a boy since he felt he did not bond with his own father. It was like a new beginning and another chance for both of us, and it just felt as if it were meant to be. We tossed around different ideas for both a girl and boy and finally settled on Andrew James.

I started to feel Andrew early on with flutter-like movements. We had just completed a major project in our lives and already began to begin another. We had a new baby to prepare for, and there was no manual! I was high on life, and Andrew became the focus of my life and also my motivation to finish my degree. I knew that in order for me to be the best mom I could be, I had to obtain my college education because that is what I would want for my Andrew. I would want my child to establish a higher level of education in class. I wanted to complete my studies so I could teach Andrew all I knew and guide him to the best of my ability.

I quickly experienced morning sickness and was also placed on bedrest a few months into the pregnancy. I took a semester off from school at the main campus and registered for the evening program closer by with a shorter commute. I was limited to the evening programs, but it was still more conducive than attending the main campus with public transportation. It was hard for me to sit still at home, and laundry and dishes were not going to wash themselves. I tried to rest as often as I could, but there was still so much to do. Joe was out of the home often, focused on work so I took on the main responsibility of the housework. The doctor told me I had to ease up on the housework because I was dilated at five months, and this baby was eager to meet the world.

Thankfully, Andrew was only born a week early and was a very healthy child. Joe was able to bring me to the hospital but not able to stay during birth. There was a very cold side to Joe I would soon find out. It didn't upset me that Joe wasn't present in the delivery room until a few days later. I think I became a little more disconnected than ever before to Joe but more connected to baby Andrew James. I turned down the epidural to only find myself in excruciating pain that became unbearable. Somehow, I knew there was a reason for all this pain and suffering. I knew there was a reason for this sacrifice and a reason why I had to have this child and share him with the world. I eventually asked the anesthesiologist to inject my spine with the epidural because the pain intensity increased, but I was scared and alone. I wanted someone smart to oversee the doctor, and I trusted Joe. I wanted him to just be there with me, but Joe was nowhere to be found. Joe said he had to take a call out of the hospital, but he never came back until a few hours later.

We already established that my parents would show at the hospital once the baby was born. It was my female ob-gyn who held my hand during that pain and remained in the room for the course. I felt excruciating pain because the epidural was injected too late. This pain overtook my body, and I was at a loss for words. I felt this pain all through my body, and it seemed as though I was literally going to die. I grabbed the side of the bed rail and curled up my body to one side until the pain finally diminished. The epidural started to take effect twenty minutes later, and I could finally straighten out my legs. Joe popped in to find Andrew's head halfway out of my vaginal area. I was almost there! I was almost a mom! My life would change forever in the next few moments only as a result of a beautiful baby boy, my son! I heard "Waaah," and I took one glance over and immediately fell in love! Joe was more concerned with how many toes and fingers Andrew had while I was infatuated with the feeling that overcame me and my body and soul as a mom to this innocent and precious baby boy.

Andrew looked just like Joe, only with darker hair. He was absolutely beautiful with gorgeous skin that lit up the room! We immediately connected, and I couldn't bear to be without him for a minute. The nurse gave me a bottle to give to Andrew, and he latched right on. I couldn't breastfeed, even though I made an attempt. I was too nervous to allow my child to feed off my breast, and it didn't feel natural. My breasts were in severe pain, and I didn't want anyone to touch them. Still, this was a new beginning for me, and I finally felt a LOVE like no other. It was a kind of innocent and genuine love I never experienced before. Andrew was my precious angel that taught me unconditional LOVE.

I was the luckiest mom alive, and I finally found a reason to stay motivated and to live for. I continued to work for Joe's business and finish class while tending to this child. Joe was not in agreement for me to finish class, but he knew that was my goal before we were married. Joe gave me a hard time about class and said I didn't need my education. I was already set up and my education was a waste of money and time.

Soon after, Joe began to create disruption in my life by ringing the phone every fifteen to twenty minutes or so throughout the day. Joe also would cause havoc if I didn't immediately answer his calls and yell at me or search for me by contacting my family members. I started to feel more like a child instead of a partner who was reprimanded often if I wasn't as responsive as Joe expected me to be. It became more and more difficult to tend to a baby, focus on my studies, and tend to Joe. Still, I was determined and found the time to get my studies in with Andrew. I would even drive around in the car with Andrew in the car seat until he would fall asleep just so I could gain study time for a test. I realized my life became harder instead of easier, but I hung on for my dear life. I enjoyed school, and I was eager to learn because of everything I wasn't taught in life. I had to start somewhere, and a college degree was an awesome foundation to have. None of my immediate family members had a college degree, but I was determined to be the first, and it was important to my mom. I was determined to succeed so I can help all those around me in need. I became a little distant from Joe because I was not impressed by his lack of support of my education even though we agreed that I would finish at my earliest convenience.

One day, out of the clear blue, Joe called me from the office phone to tell me the feds just left his office!

I screamed, "Whaaat?"

Joe said they appeared unannounced and questioned him. I asked what it was over, and he said a client check. I was confused. Joe said, long story short, he received a check in the amount of over two hundred thousand deposited into his account. Apparently, Joe knew nothing about this deposited check by his operations manager, but I found that hard to believe. It made a lot more sense to me why Joe thought he could spend the way he did. Joe had used all the funds in the account and had to return all the money or he would wind up in jail according to the feds. We had to sell our second home on the Bayfront so Joe could pay back the monies. Thankfully, we made a great investment, and Joe didn't have to serve time. I began to question Joe more and more, and I no longer had the same level of trust for him. How could someone totally pin a deposit on his own employee without any knowledge of it? It was at that very moment when I realized Joe could do the same to me at any given time as his employee. Our relationship began to dwindle, and Joe felt it. Joe wasn't my focus, and he knew it. I became aggravated at the lack of support and inconsideration for my quiet focus time on my studies. Joe became needy and demanding all day, and his annoying behavior gradually became worse. One evening, I even spotted Joe checking up on me at class because I looked out the class window to find him zoom past my classroom by surprise. I wasn't sure what he was doing there, and it didn't place me at ease. I felt like I was stalked all throughout the day and now even at class! I couldn't get a few minutes of alone time to breathe, and it was quite disturbing. I didn't know how much longer I could carry on under these circumstances, but I tried until I broke down.

I lost weight and became thinner than ever before from all the daily demands. I was anxious from a feeling of walking on eggshells and knowing that either way no matter what I did, I was wrong. I became OCD with my home from a sense of disruption in my life and not knowing what to do or how to resolve it. I became mad and distant as a result of Joe's constant criticism. I was tired of being belittled for everything I did. I was turned off by Joe constantly mocking me for anything and everything, such as a certain style of hat I wore or pair of shoes of my choice. I was sick of being told I couldn't sing and I wasn't smart enough or strong enough to make it out in the real world. I was treated and spoken to as second class. I was tired of Joe making my family and friends unwelcome in our home. I was sick of feeling like I had no outlet or sense of peace in my life. I was frustrated by all the manipulation tactics when I confronted Joe. I wanted to discuss how I felt and how hurtful he was at times, but he just denied it all and made up one excuse after another. I was scared that every move I made was being closely watched which I would later be reprimanded for by Joe. I wasn't sure if Joe was spying on me or the feds, but I felt watched and I didn't particularly care for it. Even if it was an innocent visit to my mom's for lunch, I was questioned and mocked for it.

My ideas quickly were shut down and my creativity was stifled. My mom and I had an idea we wanted to pursue in real estate, but we were deterred from all the aggravation it caused us by Joe's fears or envy. Not only was my idea quickly shut down, but I was reprimanded for it and told that I had a husband now to work with and I shouldn't be involved in any business transactions with my mom. I felt like any move became problematic, whether it was large or small. Even if my next move consisted of lunch with my friends, I was told they weren't real friends and I was better than them. I was quickly bogged down with so much aggravation for every single move I made that it was just more peaceful and easier not to go out with friends and disconnect myself. I felt like I walked on eggshells and my head started spinning. I really couldn't live as I chose. I felt like I couldn't live according to the way Tania wanted to, and I wasn't sure how much longer I could take. Life became argumentative and draining. It was all too much at one time, and I needed someone to help me find a way out of this dark tunnel. Joe began to express his temper when he came home early one day from work and asked "where the fuck" I had been. I told him I was busy, raising a child, and he went to grab my cell phone to search through it. I immediately tried to stop him, but his anger became elevated and he pushed me down the hallway. I told him that I would place a call over to the local police station if he ever placed his arms on me again. I don't think Joe expected me to say that, so he quickly apologized and swore it would never happen again. Joe begged me not to call the police and said he was so sorry. I was so stressed I lit up a cigarette on our back deck, and I didn't smoke on a regular basis. Since Joe did not approve of me smoking, he locked me out and raised his middle finger. I knocked and knocked all night until he let me in the house. I was so hurt, and I quickly thought about the past and experienced flashbacks. I thought about how my father locked my brother and sister out of the home after school. I thought of how hungry my brother and sister probably were after school, but they couldn't get in the house to eat dinner.

The next day, Joe came home drunk for the first time in front of me. That evening brought memories of my dad, and I saw a similar type of behavior within Joe. Joe was acting more strange than ever, and he started playing his guitar and sang to me in our bedroom a song by Eric Clapton.

You Look Wonderful Tonight

It's late in the evening, she's won-
  dering what clothes to wear
She puts on her makeup and
  brushes her long blonde hair
And then she asks me, "Do I look
  all right?"
And I say, "Yes, you look wonderful tonight."

We go to a party and everyone
  turns to see
This beautiful lady that's walking
  around with me
And then she asks me, "Do you
  feel all right?"
And I say, "Yes, I feel wonderful
  tonight."

I feel wonderful tonight because I
  see the love light in your eyes
And the wonder of it all
Is that you just don't realize how
  much I love you

It's time to go home now
And I've got an aching head
So I give her the car keys and she
  helps me to bed

And then I tell her, as I turn out
    the light
I say, "My darling, you were won-
    derful tonight
Oh my darling, you were won-
    derful tonight."

I felt uneasy and confused. I finally broke down and told Joe that I couldn't live under these circumstances any more. There was something completely off but still... I couldn't figure out what it was. Joe responded by telling me that he was sick.

Joe said, "I am sicker than you'll ever know! It's best that you just go because you would only stay to try to heal me, and I can't be healed, Tania. You are a healer, Tania...but you can't heal me. I know this because I already tried to heal and others have tried to help me too, but they couldn't. You would only stay with me to try to help me so just leave. But know that if you must leave me, I will make your life a living hell, and I won't make it easy for you to go."

What was Joe talking about? I never saw Joe act like this. I wasn't sure how such a strong man could act so helpless. Still, I couldn't quite place my finger on a reason for all this madness. I was no psychiatrist nor did I fully understand the human mind. I was hoping for another answer such as, "It will all be okay. I promise we can work this out. We will go for therapy and place all this behind us."

I was hoping for a different reaction or response, but how could I trust Joe again? How could someone love me as much as Joe said he did but not want to try to make our marriage work. I resented Joe for his selfish behavior. Joe told me to leave and take our baby Andrew with me to stay at my mom's for a while. I still wasn't convinced it was over. I left for my mom's home in hopes that a break would do us all well, but it only got worse.

Chapter 4

The Wind beneath My Wings

I came home one day to pick up some belongings and found Joe half-naked partying by himself with stimulants in our home office. I walked into the laundry room to find a ripped white tank top for women with a clothespin on the side, and that only separated us more. Was there a hooker in my home? I was mortified, but at the same time, I became attracted to other male associates.

I felt an attraction to the idea of a normal man in a loving relationship, and there was one in particular I had my eye on. Still, I thought he was normal and in a much better place than I at that time. I had a long way to get where this gentleman was. I took one look at this handsome, stark, and tall gentleman when he entered the room and passed my desk with a manly scent of cologne. I wanted to melt into his arms! Maybe it was the way he spoke in front of the class or maybe it was the way he sat one seat over and directly behind me. I could sense he had his eye on me, too, and it was hard to focus. I felt so protected when I took one glance at his ankle. It was INSTANT! I thought to myself, *Now that is someone you so strive to marry!* Was I feeling like this just because my relationship was so difficult from the very beginning? Every time he walked by me, I would shy away. I didn't know him very well, but I wanted to get to know him. I was still married, soon to be a single mom, with a lot to overcome before I could even consider a solid relationship again. I was also struggling with adjusting to leaving my beautiful home behind and a lavish lifestyle with a child. I felt like I was heading in reverse and all my hard work just slipped away.

I stopped back in our home to grab a few items, but Joe wasn't home. I thought it would be fine to stay the night with Andrew until Joe came home. Joe said he wanted me to get the fuck out and he demanded that I did so in rage. Joe also threatened to contact DYFUS on me for bathing our child and snapping a photo. The photo was extremely innocent, and there were no visible body parts. Joe just wanted to continue with his tactics. We began to argue, and I became stubborn to leave. I didn't understand why I had to leave when I had the child in the home, but my mom and sister Julia begged me to just pack my bags and leave for her place since it was safer. I had visions of Joe snapping a wire or hurting me in the middle of the night especially when he threatened anyone who came close to me. I had nightmares and started watching over my shoulder everywhere I went. I became a paranoid mess and always felt as if

Joe could pop up behind me at any given time and potentially hurt me.

Joe and I had equity built in the home which is why I realized Joe stopped paying the mortgage and the car lease payment. I received a letter in the mail that our home was in the process of a pre-foreclosure due to nonpayment of our mortgage for several months. Joe didn't want me to walk away with any amount of money, and he clearly would rather bite off his own nose in spite of his face. I will never forget Joe's words when he told me I was nothing without him and I could never make it out there alone. Luckily, we found a buyer within the next two months to take over our beautiful home. I was so sad to leave this home behind and part with all the hard effort placed within it. I knew I had no choice but to move on or matters would only worsen. I was completely crushed, but I knew my safety was more important than the lavish lifestyle.

I became more and more uncertain of my life, and everyone around it. Derik, my handsome crush, and I warmed up a bit after a few conversations. Our group study decided it was time to head out for a quick bite after class. Derik decided to join us so I asked him if he would order a drink like the rest of us after class, but he said he couldn't and he was on the job. I was confused by his response but didn't pry. We began to flirt here and there and even saw each other at a group study. I was invited to a second group study with another classmate, but she couldn't make it, so it was just this handsome man and me when he made a real move! I was totally taken back and definitely not ready for a commitment! I knew something was off when he popped in a sexy DVD with a blonde chick half-naked in his disk player after our quick study recap. He said that woman was his type, and her hair and face resembled mine but she had much larger breasts than me. In fact, she had beautiful large breasts that popped out of her *Baywatch* bathing suit that even I was intrigued.

Derik placed his arm around me and leaned in to kiss me. I wasn't as receptive, but I didn't complain. Derik looked deep into my eyes and said, "What's wrong? Did you not like that?" as I could see his hand shake. I told him that I was just taken by surprise and not expecting a kiss.

We enjoyed a LandShark beer and called it a night. I wasn't a regular beer drinker, but I could handle one or two as long as it was poured in a glass and I was in Derik's company. Derik made sure my beer was poured into a glass for me.

Derik asked me to dinner a week or two later, and I accepted. Derik and I met at his house and then walked over to the sushi restaurant. I was so nervous that Joe could be watching us and hurt me but more worried he could hurt Derik. I couldn't concentrate on our conversation because all I could think of was Joe popping in on us unexpectedly, and I was afraid, but I tried not to show it.

We left the restaurant and walked back to Derik's house. We made out on his sofa under a warm brown blanket. I felt comfortable in Derik's arms, but I knew this couldn't be the right time. I still felt like someone was watching me. I had doubts and fears that crept up, and I needed time to heal. I felt like Derik was secretive and even watching me when I wasn't supposed to know it. Derik told me he wouldn't have access to a phone because he was going away to a retreat, and I knew he wasn't being honest with me. Once again, I felt smothered, and it quickly brought back memories of a feeling of being entrapped inside, so I knew it couldn't be right.

Soon after, I was asked out by a renowned plastic surgeon in the local area, and I accepted. I was running away from an unwanted feeling I couldn't control. I also knew that I had to heal from my past but also find myself. At the same time, I was at battle with pressures from men around me. I had a feeling Derik knew from his strange behavior, and it made me feel like I was once again being invaded upon. After all I had overcome, I knew it was bad timing and I became annoyed at Derik, and I was quickly turned off.

Eventually, I apologized, but we never discussed a relationship or a commitment. I guess we were just kids considering all the above mentioned. Still, I knew Derik was hurting, and I couldn't just let it go. I had to apologize to his face and hope that he accepted my apology. I made an attempt to call him, but he never answered. I left him a message, but there was no callback.

Finally, I drove down to his house and knocked on his door. Derik answered the door, but he didn't look happy. I apologized for upsetting him. Derik said it was okay, and he wasn't upset. I knew deep down, when I glanced at his squinty eyes, Derik was still upset and that upset me. I could tell I was not welcome because Derik was super short with me and quickly shut me out. I left Derik's house, and we never spoke again.

Timing just wasn't on our side, but they say people come into your life for a reason. Sometimes that reason is a blessing or a lesson. That night, I learned I was not ready for a successful relationship. I learned I didn't want to be untrusted nor did I want someone to sneak behind my back secretly and spy on me. I wanted a two-way relationship, with communication and understanding. I wanted to form an old, traditional-style relationship and get to know one another like our parents did, face-to-face. Thoughts raced on and off of a new relationship, and I felt shattered. What was wrong with me? Was I ever going to be normal again? I couldn't think straight especially when I drove so I listened to music and sang with Kelly Clarkson to "Breakaway."

> Da-da-da, un, da-da
> Da-da-da, un da-da
>
> Grew up in a small town
> And when the rain would fall
>   down
> I'd just stare out my window
> Dreaming of what could be

And if I'd end up happy
I would pray

Trying hard to reach out
But when I tried to speak out
Felt like no one could hear me
Wanted to belong here
But something felt so wrong here
So I prayed (I would pray)
I could breakaway

I'll spread my wings and I'll learn
    how to fly
I'll do what it takes 'til I touch
    the sky
And I'll make a wish, take a
    chance, make a change
And breakaway

Out of the darkness and into the
    sun
But I won't forget all the ones
    that I love
I'll take a risk, take a chance,
    make a change
And breakaway
Da-da-da...

Still, I often thought of Derik and what a true
gentleman he really was. I remembered how he held
my hand as we walked down to the sushi restaurant

and how he wanted me to walk on the right side of the sidewalk so I was protected. I remembered how he opened the door for me and picked up the tab at the restaurant. I thought of how he kept me warm with his blanket and offered to make me something to eat if I was hungry. I loved how I felt with Derik, but I knew I had to heal and literally find myself. I knew Derik also knew after he told me to seek therapy but not in a demeaning manner. I don't think I would have sought out therapy if it wasn't for meeting Derik. Derik was never demeaning to me, and I missed him every so often. I thought of Derik very often and always wished him well, but above all, I wished him love.

I took on a finance internship over the summer to gain experience in the field I planned to pursue. so I had to get some rest for the morning. The internship was nonpaid, but it introduced me to all aspects of the finance department for a large accounting firm.

I was working on a compensation project when I received a message from my mom on my cell phone. "Tania, call me back as soon as you receive the message. The police were here, looking for you! The police said you must contact them immediately. Otherwise, they would show up at your place of work."

My heart sunk, and I could no longer concentrate on the compensation project I began that day. I told my supervisor that I had to head out a bit early as there was a personal situation at home that needed my attention. I left work that day confused, scared, and anxious.

When I arrived home that evening, I immediately called the local PD. When I called the police station, the dispatcher asked me to stop in at the station as soon as possible. I was shocked, and I felt humiliated. My mom offered to join me for support.

I entered the police station and identified myself. The police officer took me in the back room to inform me that there had been a terroristic threat call charge against me, and I would need to appear in court. That evening, I realized I would need my family's support more than I had intended.

I appeared in court with a family friend who just happened to be an attorney. The attorney agreed to help me with a small charge and a group dinner on me. Still, the attorney said he had to know if I made the threat against my soon-to-be ex-husband out of anger so he could properly represent me. I swore I would never say such a thing. I barely cursed, but I felt like I may just so begin to do so. I was in tears, and I felt ashamed for something I never said. Joe never did appear in court that day, and the charge was dismissed by the municipal judge.

That weekend was spent with the attorney, his buddy, and my two sisters and me over dinner and drinks. I literally felt like I was living inside a television or some fiction movie but it was a HORROR FLICK. Not only was this terroristic threat charge entirely made up, but this dinner post court almost felt staged. I began to question if all this was really real or just a bad dream. When would I awake? When would my life finally be normal? Why would Joe do this to me? I couldn't fathom how someone could stoop to this immoral level. And…what about dinner? My mind began to race. Was I supposed to entertain this attorney and his friend, like come up with some funny story, or was I supposed to introduce his friend to one of my friends or was I supposed to just dress cute? This was all so new to me, and I felt foreign. This attorney couldn't possibly be interested in me since he was married, but what about his friend? Was this a way to just get to know each other a little better? I was just going to go with the flow, and my sisters would be there to back me up. Dinner was delicious and cheaper than I actually thought it would be. No one overate because we had to save some room for drinks. The steak and seafood were absolutely delicious, and the ambiance was so beautiful and relaxing.

Drinks followed dinner, at a local lounge nearby. I was able to get to know my attorney friend a bit more and his friend as well. His friend was actually very handsome with a Ken-type build. It was funny because I could have fit the Barbie description that evening alongside him in my jean miniskirt. The attorney's friend, Christian, and I discussed potentially meeting up someday for dinner alone when all the commotion passed behind me, but he didn't seem like anything would be rushed and I was totally onboard. I was ready to call it a night when the attorney, Marc, suggested we hang out in his room on the balcony nearby. I was not surprised the boys booked a room since it was a drive for both of them to head back, but I was not super interested in prolonging the night. In opposition to my opinion were my sisters vote to continue the evening.

I was usually first to end the night early because I loved my sleep and early mornings, but I knew it wasn't often we all got the chance to hang together so I went along with the flow. Both my sisters Lina and Julia came out in my favor. I agreed to hang a bit longer. Besides, we were all together. What could possibly go wrong?

The night became a little weird. My eldest sister, Julia, may have felt like an outcast because she didn't receive the majority of attention. The attorney, Marc, started to flirt a bit more than expected with my sister Lina by sitting practically on top of her chair next to her! Christian started flirting a bit more with me and became a bit too touchy-feely. My sister Julia caught wind and absolutely FLIPPED HER LID. Was she just being super protective, or was there something in her drink that made her turn into a woman in rage? Was she jealous this handsome man was flirting with me and not her? Some things, we will never know.

Julia started yelling, "Hey, you! Get the f——off my sister! I know what you want to do!"

I was mortified and he was shocked. We weren't sure exactly where Julia's head was that evening, but it just wasn't realistic to believe anything other than a flirtatious act would have taken place if we were all together in the room. In any event, I walked out the door in total embarrassment, and my two sisters soon followed. I could still hear them screaming at Marc and Christian on their way out of the apartment building. It was a night I could never forget, and I never did speak to either of them since.

The next time I saw Joe was when he had the right to exercise parenting time. I had to meet him in his local residential town just so his son could spend time with him, but it was on his terms. The court-ordered parenting schedule was never followed because Joe came up with excuse after excuse as to why he couldn't make the time set, then demanded time when it was convenient for him. I realized this was a major control struggle Joe battled. It was just easier and less confrontational to go with Joe's demands than to fight it. Joe came up to my door in a mad rush with a red face demanding that I open my door. I unlocked the door to let Joe in and opened the back door to grab Andrew out of his car seat when Joe spat on my head. I assumed this anger from Joe came from his loss at the recent court appearance. I didn't mind when Joe was not available to spend time with Andrew because I felt safer with him in my arms, and I worried too often when he wasn't.

Graduation day came, and I felt so accomplished and empowered! I was the first child in my family to obtain my bachelor's degree as a college graduate. I made my mom even more proud than I was. There were days I wasn't quite sure how I concentrated or stayed focused with a baby, but I did it. Somehow

I knew it was all worth it, and I would carry this knowledge with me throughout my professional and personal life ahead! I was so grateful for all my professors and the pleasant students I met. I knew how hardworking and tired these students were as working adults, and I was honored to sit beside them in class. I was excited for this new chapter ahead, although I wasn't quite sure where the path ahead would take me. I thought of enrolling in a master's program, and then even law school, but with my current situation and all the oppression from Joe, I had to be realistic. I knew I couldn't parent my child as the main sole residential parent as the main focus AND succeed in a master's program. I knew I would miss too much of my child's early years, and we would miss each other too much. Who would take care of Andrew while I was gone or concentrating on work?

I tossed around the idea of working for the FBI, but my mom said it was no place for a mother of a child to work in. I really wanted to work in finance, but I was too affected to sit still in an office all day. I had developed OCD, amongst other issues, and I felt the urge to keep on running. I wanted to run away from something completely out of my control, but I didn't know how to.

I woke up the next morning and glanced out my other kitchen door to find my truck literally being towed away. Oh my gosh! I just lost my home, but now my vehicle was just taken away without any notice! I cried to my mom, but she said it was just a car, and we could get a new one. I found out my car payment was in default and all the mail was sent to the old address. I had to pay off the balance before I could drive my vehicle again. The vehicle cost me thousands of dollars in back pay, but I felt I had no choice at that time. Everything moved so quickly, and I was still adjusting to a new life with many losses. The thought of concentrating in an office for work made me anxious. I had too much on my mind, and so much more to overcome. Joe wasn't gonna make this easy for me. In fact, Joe told me that I would never make it on my own, and I was nothing without him. I was determined to prove him wrong and do just the opposite. How dare he question my capabilities? I was hardworking and smart, and I believed in the fight for a good cause. I began my job search and found a position in business development for a pharmaceutical lab. The salary wasn't bad to start, and I could enjoy that flexibility I needed as a mom to my son. I could run my own schedule and didn't have to sit in one place. Everything else would have to run around my work as a parent, and I stuck to my guns.

Andrew needed me now more than ever. I wanted Andrew to have the guidance and support I felt every child needed and not exactly what I or Joe claimed he had. I wanted Andrew to have a childhood filled with love and support, one that he would think back on and smile. I wanted Andrew to have a fair start in life, one of which I did not have. I knew I could give that to him as long as I was healthy, and with the support of my parents to back me up while I was at work. I knew I could give Andrew a nice childhood despite Joe's behavior directed to me, as long as he could financially assist me with support for Andrew. I was on my way to be the best parent I could be! In fact, we were already on our way to an awesome childhood, or at least I thought we were.

I found my strength in my mom's loving arms, and she became the wind beneath my wings. My mom gave me the support I needed to parent Andrew and continue this fight. I knew in my heart that if my mom could survive her tormented life, then I could overcome, too, with her support! Did she ever know that she was my hero? I may have had glory, but she was the one with all the strength. A beautiful face to hide her pain. I could fly higher than an eagle, but my mom was the wind beneath my wings.

Chapter 5

The Miracle

My faith in miracles was strengthened through the eyes of my son at birth. Andrew and I started throwing a bouncy ball at just six months old. Andrew would love to sit on top of our little mound outside on the grassy hill while I sat at the bottom and giggle every time he caught the ball. Most children say "Dada" as their first word, but Andrew said, "Baaahlll!" Every time Andrew said ball, his eyes would get larger, and he would pack on that Kool-Aid smile I could never forget. It was when Andrew's eyes first glistened when I knew he had a love for the ball.

Andrew and I took Gymboree classes together for socialization, but he never did love that parachute. Maybe it was just overwhelming for Andrew when we all picked up the parachute and it made a swooshing sound as it swooped its way back down to the music. I do remember Andrew enjoyed climbing up and down and moving his body through the tunnels in the baby gym. Andrew would turn his baby head around and smile then giggle and head back out there.

Andrew had so much energy, and he never napped throughout the day. I had to drive Andrew in the car around the corner just to get a break or even to catch up on schoolwork or study for a test! Somehow, we made it all happen, and I never missed a day filled with joy with baby Andrew. We strolled around the neighborhood with the baby carriage and made our way to the local parks. We went shopping with Grandma Jana and ate at the finest luncheons. Andrew drove in the finest cars with his dad, and he never left home without a binky for his mouth. We drove to Disney World as the excitement of our baby overtook us! We climbed, crawled, sang, laughed, and cried together. I was the happiest mommy alive, and I was so blessed to be Andrew's mom! There wasn't a day when Andrew disappointed me, and I fell head over heels. Words couldn't express my gratitude for Andrew, but every time I heard these lyrics, I thought of my love for my Son and how he made me feel when he was born:

A New Day Has Come
Celine Dion

A new day
A new day
I was waiting for so long
For a miracle to come
Everyone told me to be strong

Hold on and don't shed a tear
Through the darkness and good
    times
I knew I'd make it through
And the world thought I had it
    all
But I was waiting for you

(Hush, love)
I see a light in the sky
Oh, it's almost blinding me
I can't believe
I've been touched by an angel
    with love

Let the rain come down and wash
    away my tears
Let it fill my soul and drown my
    fears
Let it shatter the walls
For a new sun
A new day has come

Where it was dark now there is
    light
Where there was pain, now there
    is joy
Where there was weakness, I
    found my strength
All in the eyes of a boy

Hush now
I see a light in the sky
Oh it's almost blinding me
I can't believe I've been touched
    by an angel
With Love

Let the rain come down
And wash away my tears
Let it fill my soul
And drown my fears
Let it shatter the walls
For a new Sun
A new day has come
Oh, oh oh

Hush, now
I see a light in your eyes
All in the eyes of a boy (A new
    day)
I can't believe I've been touched
    by an
Angel, with love (A new day)
Oh, oh
Hush, now

A new day
Hush, now
A new day

Andrew was a miracle baby and my reason to carry on. I pledged to love, protect, and serve this baby boy till my last dying breath as his mother. We built a close bond and unconditional love that words or lyrics still could never fully describe. I remained on a natural high from a feeling of spending time with this child. We played on Andrew's new beautiful swing set, and we swam in our beautiful built-in pool. We visited parks, beaches, friends, and family any chance we could.

Time flew by, and it was time for mommy to begin work and Andrew to begin school. We both experienced a little separation anxiety, but it was more obvious to see on Andrew's face through his tears when I dropped him off at school. It broke my heart to part with Andrew, but I knew we had to carry on and begin to separate and overcome our anxieties. I couldn't wait to see Andrew's smile after work, and he was all I looked forward to after a hard-earned day's pay. Although I was exhausted, I became accustomed to my second role and responsibility to Andrew. I really didn't have a choice. Andrew and I spent dinner time together followed by homework Monday to Friday. We read and worked on class-work so Andrew would understand his work and be rewarded with great grades!

Travel was required for my job, and probably the toughest part was leaving Andrew. Although I knew he was in great hands with my parents, I wanted to be close to him at all times.

Andrew hopped in my suitcase one time and said, "Mommy, someday, I will travel with you, right?"

My heart melted when Andrew told me he dedicated this song to me by Phil Collins:

Can't Stop Loving You

So you're leaving in the morning
    on the early train
I could say everything's all right
And I could pretend and say
    goodbye
Got your ticket
Got your suitcase
Got your leaving smile
I could say that's the way it goes
And I could pretend and you
    won't know
That I was lying

'Cause I can't stop loving you
No I can't stop loving you
No I won't stop loving you
Why should I?

We took a taxi to the station, not
    a word was said
And I saw you walk across the
    road

For maybe the last time, I don't
    know
Feeling humble
I heard a rumble
On the railway track
And when I hear that whistle
    blow
I'll walk away and you won't
    know
That'll I'll be crying

'Cause I can't stop loving you
No I can't stop loving you
No I won't stop loving you
Why should I?

Even try, I'll always be here by
    your side
Why, why, why I never wanted to
    say goodbye
Why even try, I'll always be here
    if you change, change your
    mind

So you're leaving in the morning
    on the early train
I could say everything's alright
And I could pretend and say
    goodbye
But that would be lying

'Cause I can't stop loving you
No I can't stop loving you
No I won't stop loving you
Why should I even try?

As if it wasn't enough to see a happy beautiful smile when I greeted my baby boy, he dedicates a beautiful loving song to me. Moving forward, I would make a point to travel with my loving angel every chance I could outside of work. I knew my angel felt the same way I did about him, and we shared an everlasting love that couldn't die, no matter the distance between us, ever. My son became a part of my heart that was a miraculous and unconditional love, one like no other. A love I would hold close to my heart in the many years ahead in this lifetime.

We traveled one to two times a year, and I cherished every trip, and the time we shared with our family friends who traveled with us.

Although Andrew brought me so much joy and love to the world, I felt sad that a male partner was missing in my life. Every time I opened up to a male or attempted to get closer, I would quickly shut it down. The man wasn't Andrew's father and it didn't feel quite right. I would think of my past, and it brought me to a very negative place. I realized that my past had affected my future, and I would need to place some work into that. I turned away from anyone who made any attempt to get closer to me. This was partly because Joe continued to threaten anything potentially positive in my life and partly because my mind was not in the right state. I started therapy three times a week, and it helped me understand myself a little more. I gained a better understanding of why people mistreated innocent beings. I also read books on how to better manage difficult personalities and overcome abuse. I studied the human mind because I struggled to understand why I was mistreated and turned on in such a cruel manner for no apparent reason.

Chapter 6

I'm Loving Angels Instead

I needed a break from human interaction, but I wanted Andrew to grow up surrounded by love. Andrew was an only child, but there were times I wished he wasn't and he had a brother or sister to confide in. Andrew and I thought it might be a good time to adopt a new addition to the family. I didn't have much experience with dogs nor did I know much about them, but I knew people seemed to absolutely LOVE them! I thought it would be nice for Andrew to grow up with a dog since studies proved positive behaviors by children raised with animals. I also thought it would be nice to cuddle with a fur baby from time to time, but I had zero clue how much love I was capable of having for a nonhuman addition to the family. Andrew and I tossed around the idea of a puppy, but I had no idea what kind of dog would best suit us. *Boom*! It was an omen! A few days later, I couldn't help but notice a large poster with several photos of puppies posted on a tree with a phone number and message that read: "Call to make an appointment." I knew absolutely nothing about the breed, but I couldn't believe how adorable these puppies were. I called to make an appointment because what harm could it do to browse?

Andrew's birthday was just around the corner, and I wanted it to be a special birthday so we decided to fit a trip over into our busy baseball schedule and check out these puppies. We were able to get Jana to join us as well and feel her out.

We arrived at a large farm area on huge acreage with a barn and heavy equipment. Our drive was only about 20 minutes away from home. We were led into the second-level barn area. I recall walking around a few stacks of hay. I immediately fell in love from the moment I saw these puppies. The puppies were all caged and were climbing on the cage and each other. One was cuter than the next, and there were too many that needed a home. Andrew was set on a boy, and sure enough, the one little guy who wouldn't leave us alone happened to be a male. This little guy immediately jumped into Andrew's arms and he knew he was "The One."

Andrew said, "Mom, he's the one. Can we take him home?"

It was Andrew's tenth birthday, how could we say no? Andrew was gifted with a furry stepbrother! Although there wasn't much resemblance, their hearts were aligned, and they truly cared so much for each other. We introduced our fur baby to the family and all fell head over heels. Andrew's baby cousin Jaden would pick up our fur baby like a real baby and walk up and down the stairs with him.

Andrew gave our new member of the family the name Spike. Our baby was absolutely adorable and he loved to play, but there was also work to be done. Our baby needed to be potty-trained and checked out by the vet. I had no idea how to potty train a dog or what to feed him. The vet gave us a few tips, and we figured out the rest! I placed wee-wee pads around the home and started with a popular brand of dog food. Sure enough, we figured it out, but our fur baby never did fully train as he should have. I was focused on healing myself while Andrew was being a tween consumed with sports. I eventually made an attempt to train our fur baby, but he was a little too old, and you know that old saying, "You can't teach an old dog new tricks." I took accountability and accepted that I should have signed up for training earlier. I also regretted just adopting one baby instead of two. Our fur baby could have probably come home with his brother or sister for comfort and socialization.

Spike's first baby toy was a gray elephant, and he was used for comfort during rest and periods of sleep. It must have been the shape of the trunk on that animal toy that Spike just loved to grasp because no other toy could take his place. Spike loved to run laps around the kitchen and in the yard, and he always seemed to cuddle up next to a member of the family. Spike was the most loving, sweetest baby to the family, but he actually nipped at almost any stranger unknown to him. In fact, baby cousin Jaden made it a point to let everyone know they had to be careful. When a child would walk over to Spike and express how cute he was, Jaden would reiterate and say, "HE BITES." The parents would immediately back up their children away from Spike, especially when he grinned and showed off his teeth! Spike had a habit of showing off his teeth to anyone who walked into the house as a possible threat.

I wasn't quite sure how to make him stop biting, especially when he broke skin and scared the little ones. There were times I wished I could also control his raging bark that would strike right through you in a high-pitched tone. We later realized that he was only protecting his loved ones and that was a form of how he knew to profess his love and gratitude. Spike's eating habits were just as challenging as Andrew's because they both had fussy eating habits. The main difference was that Spike enjoyed cheese for dessert and Andrew preferred brownies. Spike's first visit with Joe during visitation with Andrew was when had his first taste of roast beef. After Spike's first visit to Joe's house, his eating habits were never the same. Not that Spike ever really loved his dog food, he now wanted to accept it as his own food even less. Spike started to really enjoy human food and later developed somewhat of an addiction to a variety of different cheese.

There wasn't a day I wished Spike away, and my love for him only grew stronger. The family followed suit, and Spike became one of us and someone we cared for and protected just like the members of the family. I could cuddle up with Spike all day long. I even took Spike out to work with me on occasions since Spike shared a similar joy as Andrew, and that was car rides. Although there wasn't much of a resemblance to Spike, he was officially the adopted addition that we absolutely loved and couldn't imagine life without. We ate together, played ball outside together, danced together, and definitely cuddled together any chance we could. Spike became the family household protector and although he wasn't very big or intimidating, he could quickly alarm you by informing you there was suspicious noise on the grounds. My deep intrigue for Spike only grew, and I wondered how this creature could carry this much weight for the love we had for him. It was almost as if Spike was sent to us during a difficult period in life, and it was just meant to be for him to love, protect, and console us when we suffered. I also noticed Spike tended to flock around the family member in deepest pain the most, like an angel. Spike didn't leave my side during the pain I carried for a year, so I sang…

Angels
Robbie Williams

I sit and wait
Does an angel contemplate my
    fate
And do they know
The places where we go
When we're gray and old

'Cause I've been told
That salvation lets their wings
   unfold

So when I'm lying in my bed
Thoughts running through my
   head
And I feel the love is dead
I'm loving angels instead

And through it all he offers me
   protection
A lot of love and affection
Whether I'm right or wrong
And down the waterfall
Wherever it may take me
I know that life won't break me
When I come to call, she won't
   forsake me
I'm loving angels instead

When I'm feeling weak
And my pain walks down a one-
   way street
I look above

And I know I've been blessed
   with love
And as the feeling grows

He breathes flesh to my bones
And when love is dead

I'm loving angels instead

I trusted Spike more than anyone else around me. I understood Spike and his good intentions. Although Spike was different, he brought comfort and joy to my family. Spike wasn't very jealous nor could he or did he bad-mouth anyone. Spike didn't inflict any pain on us nor was he ungrateful to be with us. I learned Spike wanted nothing more than our company, and he took his job as our protector very seriously. We smiled when Spike was near, and we felt a tad bit safer that he was around. I was absolutely amazed at the loyalty this furry creature carried, and I felt absolutely blessed! It finally made sense why so many families wanted a dog, including my dad many, many years ago. I found you can receive the gift of love also through something other than a human, a furry animal. I loved Spike like my child, and I began to wonder what life would be like without him when I almost lost him. I was so worried that my time with Spike was up on one cold, windy, dark, and rainy evening.

Andrew spent the night with Joe, and I was home alone. It was a cold, spring evening when Spike vanished right before my very own eyes. It wasn't like me to separate myself for too long from Spike without knowing his whereabouts. I awoke from hearing the strong winds outside to immediately look for

Spike. I called out to Spike and said, "Spike! where are you?"

I walked all around the house and along the outdoor perimeter in the rain. I couldn't believe what was happening! I just had a fence built so Spike could enjoy the backyard safely. It just so happened that Spike snuck out and in between the two panels to escape the thunder and rain. I thought about life without Spike and how sad I would be. I thought about all our memories and how much he meant to the family. I wanted to break down and call my mother like a child, but it was about 3:00 a.m., and I wasn't sure how she would help me. I caught my breath and took a moment to think. I drove in my car near the park where I knew Spike was familiar. There wasn't a car in sight in the stormy weather. I drove around and around in somewhat of a panic. Sure enough, Spike noticed my headlights on that foggy evening, and he darted at my car, soaking wet in a walk of shame. Spike looked like he was a total of 6 pounds soaking wet and was frantic. I immediately stopped the car, opened the passenger door, and demanded Spike to get in! Spike quickly turned his head down as he knew I was not happy with him. I told him that I could have lost him and he could have been killed by a car! I asked Spike what he was thinking, but there was no response back. I wrapped Spike in a blanket and held him in my arms tighter than ever the entire ride home!

Spike became such a huge importance in my life, and I protected him just as he protected my family. I wanted to keep Spike safe and secure so his fears could too subside. I knew dogs didn't live forever, but I wasn't ready to say goodbye this soon. My heart would be totally crushed. I would almost relate it to being a single mom who recently lost her son. Life just wouldn't be the same, and I wasn't ready to make another adjustment or suffer another loss. I finally fell asleep with Spike next to my side. I held his paw and fell fast asleep until I could feel he no longer wanted to feel my touch. I finally accepted that although I was single, I was not lonely or unloved. I had been blessed with love all around me, even by creatures that may have been sent from above to console us during challenging times.

Chapter 7

Comfortably Numb

I wondered why Mr. Right hadn't come long yet. What was wrong with me? Why was I the unfortunate one? Finally, I met my fiancé who didn't seem overbearing, jealous, or aggressive with me. I was introduced by a work connection to a handsome orthopedic surgeon, and we just so happened to share a romantic connection. We began to spend time, first together and then with our children. Soon after, we felt extreme pressure once again from Joe and my fiancé's ex. We tried to stay strong and hopeful for our relationship. We even had professional photos taken and announcements were sent out after my hand was asked in marriage in New York City. My fiancé's family didn't seem too excited for us, and maybe it was because they knew we both weren't ready for marriage. I was healing from a personal injury and divorce while my fiancé was healing from a bad divorce and financial issues.

Joe threatened my fiancé and caused havoc for attempting a relationship with me. This time, Joe also placed pressure on Andrew for spending time with my fiancé and me. I felt so guilty for being in this new relationship, but I shouldn't have. Why did I feel like I shouldn't have been there with Andrew? I thought of how I could spend time with a new partner when you are a parent and his father is threatening you and your partner not to do so. I started to lose faith in a relationship since every attempt I made to share love was destroyed. There were times I felt like giving up as a parent, and I became depressed. I loved Andrew with all my heart, but I knew that I needed an adult kind of romantic love and Joe just wasn't going to allow that to happen as long as I had to care for Andrew in my life. Still, I had to continue the fight for Andrew and make him my focused priority.

Eventually, I found my fiancé involved with inappropriate texting with another woman, and so it was confirmed we weren't ready for a commitment. I felt more pain than I was already in, and I didn't know that was possible. We decided to cut our ties and part ways. I was struck by a vehicle and suffered from a lot of physical damage shortly before I met my fiancé. Not only did I have a mental state to work on, but now also my physical body to repair. I became comfortably numb from all the pain. Life became more challenging. I thought back about Mitzi's reading. I began to understand what Mitzi meant by my hand would be asked in marriage more than once, but only with two men in my life. I was devastated but remained hopeful. I assumed there was someone else for me, but I had to be patient. I had to accept it just wasn't my time. I became more and more comfortable being the outcast. My entire life was based upon me feeling as if I were different and a fish out of water. Life seemed so unfair to me but I had to stay in faith, be grateful for my blessings and keep on smiling. Really, what other choice did I have? I made it this far...

I continued to support Andrew in his athletic interests and attended almost every game. Andrew became an awesome baseball player, and he soon developed quick reflexes and a sharp eye. Andrew even played on a recreation team along with two travel teams at one time. It was great to see Andrew play the most important positions in the field along with starting player position. My time became totally consumed by Andrew's athletics. I knew my father's athletic capabilities lived through my son! I just knew it would! Andrew's team needed him, and he was taught commitment. I enjoyed every possible moment on the field but never felt like I fit in. Was I ever gonna have time for a relationship with a partner ever again? I wasn't married nor did I have the support of a husband, and it didn't always make me feel so good. My relationships never seemed to pan out, and I was dealing with more opposition from Joe than ever. I had to see Joe appear at Andrew's game, and it made me cringe at times. You just never knew what mood you would get. Sometimes Joe would say hello, and other times, he would snub me. Sometimes, Joe would flirt with all the women in front of me, and it was most likely to spite me. Sometimes Joe would bring a female friend to see Andrew play ball, and other times, it was his dog who came along. Nonetheless, every time was uncomfortable for me, but I will never forget the embarrassment I felt one game when Joe called me a fucking whore in front of many parents. Joe never made Andrew or I feel comfortable around him because you just never knew how badly you would be treated. Still, Andrew remained the apple of my eye, and there was no way I would allow anyone to interfere with his future capabilities.

One day out the blue, Joe called me to tell me he heard my engagement was off, and he knew it wouldn't work. I am not sure the fact that Joe threatened to drag my fiancé through his tiled glass in his office by his neck if he didn't stay away from his son, Andrew, had nothing to do with the falling out! Joe begged me to just a conversation over coffee. Of course, I initially declined, but of course, Joe wouldn't accept no for an answer so he appeared at my parents' home over and over again until I finally agreed to just coffee.

Ten years had passed, and Joe told me he wanted another chance at our family. Of course, Joe said he was sorry and he realized his mistakes. Joe asked if he could make it up to me and care for Andrew in a home together the way it should have been. Of course, I was in love with the idea of family life together, especially for Andrew; and I wanted all the chaos to come to a complete halt, so I eventually agreed. I agreed to a second chance at our family for us but mainly for Andrew. It was only fair that Andrew got to know his father a little better by living together so he could eventually form an opinion of his own. Besides, I had nothing to lose. Every relationship I attempted was destroyed mostly the reason from Joe either directly or indirectly. I was in pain, both mentally and physically. I could barely make it through the workday and then parent Andrew as my second job when I arrived home. I literally felt like I was at the lowest point in my life, crawling on the floor. Thankfully, I was living at my parent's home for support during my pain with my accident. Since Joe never made his child support payments on time, it was safest to stay with my parents so I could make ends meet. Joe just wouldn't quit and let me move on, so I caved in. Andrew was the happiest kid alive, and he told me his wish finally came true and that was to live as a family together. My heart melted, and I was so happy for us. I was able to forgive the past and attempt to move forward. I felt empowered in some way as if I became even closer to my higher power for the forgiveness of all the pain bestowed upon me.

We moved into a rental community in the same town as my parents' home so Andrew could finish up middle school with his friends. I found a community that allowed pets for our dogs to visit. We furnished our condo with mostly the same furniture as we had previously. We were the same family, but this time around, things were slightly different. It was exactly ten years later, and Joe drank alcohol now, and sometimes, more than he should. I had high hopes he would eventually stop or at least slow down. Our place was smaller, and the community wasn't quite the same as our previous one, but it would do fine for temporary purposes. We didn't have the square feet room we once did nor did we have a pool for the kids. We didn't have the parking or the privacy we once had nor did we own the place. We owed a rent check every month, but it was a clean place to call our own with our family, and I was grateful to give us a chance once again. I wasn't as healthy as I once was, and we were all ten years older. I was grateful to be alive although I suffered from so much pain in my back and neck. I had received multiple kinds of treatments for the pain, but nothing seemed to cure the real underlying pain.

After several years in an insurance battle, I was ready to undergo major spine surgery. I was frightened, but I could no longer live in this pain, managing the pain I felt as a working mother. I needed to make a drastic change in order to gain my quality of life back. I came across a laser spine surgery commercial marketing minimally invasive surgery in the New York area. This commercial immediately caught my attention, and Joe and I thought it couldn't hurt me to make an appointment for a consultation. Joe drove me to the appointment, and he supported the surgical procedure. After several tests and meeting with a few physicians at the laser center, I received great news! I couldn't believe I was a candidate for a minor laser procedure! Why didn't anyone inform me sooner? Not one surgeon directed me to consult with a surgeon for a laser procedure. Not one PT or chiro suggested I visit this facility. I was told to consult with one pain specialist after another. I had taken OTC anti-steroidal medication, pain relief patches, ice packs, heating pads, and steroid injections. I had exercised all my options including PT, chiro care, acupuncture, yoga, and rest, but not one professional suggested a minor procedure. I suffered in chronic pain day after day for a total of five years. The only relief I really had was when I overconsumed alcohol or received a steroid injection. Some lasted longer than others, but they normally would take effect for at least a few months or so. I had no idea there was such a minor procedure available for neck and back injuries. I was ecstatic not to have to undergo a major spine operation that would require an incision in my front neck. The only downside was that I had to pay for this surgery out-of-pocket since my insurance did not cover the cost. I didn't care because I was over this pain and ready to pay the financial price.

I scheduled the surgery ASAP and made arrangements to stay overnight in a local hotel to the surgery center. I woke up in the recovery room with immediate relief. Although I had felt soreness from the incision, there was an immediate lift of what felt like a heavy weight on my shoulder. I could tell Joe was shocked! I could see Joe grind his teeth as he screeched in a bittersweet moment, "You're healed! Tania, I could see your pain is gone! I can't believe it! The surgery was a success!"

I smiled as I glanced at Joe. I wondered if he was really excited for me. Joe shouted with excitement, "Let's go, Tania! Time to get you back to the room so we could make Morton steak dinner tonight. I made reservations for us for 7:30 p.m."

I walked into the steak house with my cast on my neck and a bandage on my incision the same day out of surgery. I was a bit sore from the incision, but I was happy to be there with Joe and out of the operating room with a successful surgery to talk about. I realized why Joe mistreated me at the restaurant after a beautiful dinner. Once again, he became fearful of me leaving, which could only stem from his abandonment issues from his childhood. I became a punching bag I could no longer sustain and mend together. I was already broken and not sure how much more I could take. I am not exactly sure why Joe called me a fucking cunt right at the dinner table in front of the waitress that night. I do remember his obnoxious and rude behavior yelling at me outside the restaurant.

Joe shouted, "What the fuck are you doing?" I was in the bathroom maybe a whole two minutes longer than normal. For god's sake, I just had surgery. I wondered how a person could be so cruel and heartless. I probably responded to his demands in a rather not-so-shy manner, and I asked to leave. I remember I felt as if a knife stabbed me right in my heart that evening, and I had just one more incision that night that needed to heal.

After Joe drank the entire bottle of wine plus one to himself, I knew it was time to call it a night.

Joe never did apologize for his behavior that evening. Maybe he didn't remember what he said or maybe he just never felt the pain that was inflicted upon me. Either way, I realized not much had improved over the past ten years. In fact, our living arrangement actually got worse due to Joe's drinking and partying habits. The first few months seemed great together, and Joe sounded grateful to have us all together. Joe did a pretty good job taking care of the bills and the finances, but he lacked somewhat in the communication department. The only compliment I ever heard was that I did such an amazing job raising Andrew and he was lucky to have me as his mother.

After a few months of living together, I noticed a change in Joe's moods. Joe seemed aggravated and stressed with work. This behavior brought back memories of years ago when we lived together. Joe said work really got to him, but he never did work long hours. Joe started becoming anxious and demanding when he's home. Sure enough, Joe increased his alcohol intake during the day and the verbal abuse escalated. I recall when Joe started popping in the bar by 11:00 a.m., and he wouldn't answer his phone when I rang. Was he embarrassed to tell me he was in a bar instead of on the job? Was he unhappy living with me or was he just unhappy renting in this community? I always felt like I was good company. I kept the house clean, left hot meals out on the table, and took good care of Andrew. I contributed to the bills and I made the best out of any situation. Sure, I was flawed like everyone else, but then, I wasn't sure why Joe begged me to move back together as a family when he started spending less and less time with his family.

Joe said he wasn't happy in the shit condo, and we should move next door, to the updated condo. After our one-year lease was over, we made the move only two condos down! Joe stuck me with the move, and I had minimal help. I lugged boxes and boxes of our personal belongings after I just had surgery on my spine! I noticed I was being almost treated badly in spite of just being ME!

Sometime after our second move, Joe said we had to buy a home, but he was not going to put up half the money. Was he expecting me to use my money? Something seemed off, and it was almost as if Joe was trying to trick me financially and get a hold of my savings. I quickly caught on to what seemed to be a completely unfair financial arrangement. Joe seemed disinterested in me and almost angry that I had a successful surgery. I felt like we grew apart over the next several months. Joe started even staying out in hotels or his car on some nights, and he wouldn't come home until the morning.

My birthday came up and I didn't want any special attention. My birthday was not a milestone and there was no reason for an extravagant celebration. SURPRISE! I walked into a surprise thirty-ninth birthday dinner I thought was amazing. We had a private Hibachi room with close family and friends. The cocktails were tasty, and the dinner was exquisite. Everyone showed up dressed so nicely, and we all had a fabulous time! The next morning, my sister Julia called me to tell me that Joe stopped at her house, high as a kite, pacing the house, then jumped in the shower without informing anyone. I knew what was up, sadly. By itself, it was enough to accept Joe and I had grown apart, but it wasn't easy to accept the father of my son had secretly suffered from an addiction for a very long time. Joe's employees would ring my line to ask where they were to report to, but I had no real answer for them because I didn't know where Joe was. One evening, Joe came home belligerent and demanded sex. I was never so turned off before so I had rejected Joe and locked the bedroom door behind me.

Andrew had caught mononucleosis, and I had to believe it was as a result of the chaos brought into our home once again. I homeschooled Andrew until he was ready to go back to school. Joe continued to party, but at least he paid the bills.

He came home one afternoon and shouted, "What's up with all this laundry? How much fucking laundry do you do all day? What else do you do all fucking day? Isn't there anything to eat? Go place my plate on the counter."

I said, "It's called laundry and someone has to do it." I was reprimanded for doing too much laundry! I was reprimanded for keeping a clean house! I was asked what I did all day when I was begged not to work for anyone else other than for the family business. I could tell Joe had been drinking again, and it made me nauseous.

Joe said, "Did you hear me? Grab my plate will you?"

I said, "Can you wait a minute? Can't you see I am doing the dishes?"

Joe said, "Yeah, you are always doing something."

I said, "Well, at least I do the right thing."

Joe said, "We are going to have to get married, you know."

I responded in question. "Married? You would need to seek a program before we made that move again."

Joe said, "For what? I don't have an alcohol or drug problem," as he slurred his words.

Joe was back out to the bar, and he didn't return until dark, almost killing someone in his Suburban. I found Joe passed out in his Suburban, but he didn't have a problem? Once again, Joe demanded sex later that night, and I wasn't interested. I locked the bedroom door and didn't respond to the knock.

Joe said, "Open this door and let me in, you little fucking cunt."

I was worried Andrew could hear him from down the hall. I opened the door to tell Andrew just to ignore his father if he walked into his room and shut the door. Andrew said his dad already came in and asked him odd questions with odd behavior.

Andrew said, "Mom, Dad was acting weird so I just ignored him."

My baby son was still recovering from mono with an upset stomach, and I was worried this would upset him more. Joe was pacing around the house with another open bottle of wine and a glass of red yelling about what a bitch I was with both the radio on and television blasted. I heard Joe contact his first-born son's mother and carry on an extremely inappropriate conversation right in the very same house I was living, where, by the way, we could hear words spoken. I could hear Joe speak in a very low tone as he said, "Remember when we were in the shower together and…"

I realized Joe and I grew apart, and we were not spiritually aligned. I finally accepted that we were not supposed to grow old together, and Joe was not my soul mate. Finally, I got up to say it was over, and I wanted the abuse and nonsense to stop, especially in front of my son.

Joe responded with some wise comment, and said, "I want you out of my home. I pay these bills and this is all my furniture. Go back to your mother's where you belong."

My eyes filled with tears as I said, "Okay. I will leave under one condition. This time, I want you to stay the fuck out of my life for good and let me go. Be sure you mean what you say, Joe, because this time if I leave, I am not coming back, and Andrew is coming with me."

Joe said I could leave but Andrew had to stay with him. I disagreed and told him Andrew needed to heal in a quiet home with stability. Andrew needed peace and quiet so he can study, and it wasn't fair to subject him to this madness any longer. Finally, I felt it was time to go since now Joe wanted me out, but he argued that Andrew was staying with him. I wasn't quite sure how a disrespectful, ungrateful, and irresponsible being would be able to care for a child when he couldn't care for himself.

Andrew and I packed our bags and left for my parents' home. Joe argued with me about all the furniture and told me not to touch any of his belongings even though I paid for the brand new sectional with my monies. It was easier to just leave it all and attempt to move forward once again. Andrew and I were so upset, but we knew we could not live under these circumstances much longer. I asked Andrew where he felt better about moving to, and I gave him a choice: we could either move back to my parents or in the rental home I purchased several years ago. Andrew wanted to move back to his old familiar grounds and that was my parents' home. I assumed Andrew needed a loving home to heal in once again. As upsetting as it was, I believe in my heart that it was all worth the while. Andrew was able to get to know his father a bit more, and I received confirmation it was not meant to be. I could finally rest easy and place it all behind me without a second guess. I only prayed Joe would be able to do the same.

Chapter 8

The Greatest Love of All

We left most of the furnishings and decor behind so I had to purchase an entirely new bed set for Andrew in his new room. I wasn't up for a fight over material items, and it was a losing battle. Joe told me that he would call the police if I came anywhere near his condo, and I knew I was up against a twisted plan.

Back at my parents', I tried to make the living situation as comfortable as I could, considering my sister and her family were also living with my parents. We had a full house and there was chaos at times, but we always felt protected, and we never had to long for any attention or love. We were surrounded by people who truly cared for us, and we all looked out for one another. I was still in the process of healing from my surgery so I took one day at a time. I finally found part-time work, and I was beginning my path on my career change when I received a legal packet in the mail.

Joe filed for residential custody to spite me once again even though he demanded that I get the fuck out of HIS condo, which was a rental, by the way. I was finally starting to heal my pain when BOOM! I had to hire an attorney to defend my case, but it would cost me more mental and financial drain than I already experienced. I couldn't believe this was happening! It was later found out that Joe was working hard to make contacts with local attorneys and even judges to side with him. Now it all made sense! Joe would play Santa with these fellows in high places by buying their friendship to win them over! It was all part of his plan-in-the-making. I was so frightened that Joe would find a way to manipulate this case and win residential custody for Andrew. I lost sleep, lost weight, and developed bladder issues from all the stress.

I didn't know where to begin. I thought it might be a good time to contact my divorce attorney since she handled my divorce case very well. Unfortunately, this was a different time, and I didn't have quite the same experience with her as I did many years ago! My attorney seemed more concerned with my CIS and financial statements than the well-being of my son. She questioned why I dropped the alimony she fought so hard for me to collect on. Was she just concerned about a continued fight to compensate on? I explained that Joe begged me to help him out and drop it so what was I supposed to do? I explained that my health and mental state were more important than alimony. Besides, I found a way to survive without it. I wasn't proud, but a healthy mind and safety were more important to me than a lump sum of cash. I knew some people have the potential to get violent when faced with a loss because I watched a lot of movies as a kid. My attorney still seemed more focused on my bank accounts and I began to question who she was working for.

Was my attorney really on my side? Because she didn't appear to be, and I questioned who she really represented. Not once did she question Andrew's quality of life or his surroundings. When I mentioned the drinking that was abused by Joe, her response was, "Well, don't you drink?" Well, indeed I did, but I wasn't verbally abusive when I did and that was the main difference nor did I pass out in vehicles. Only once again, I couldn't quite place my thoughts into words since my thoughts were consumed by fear. I was focused on Andrew's well-being and protecting him from a negative environment. I couldn't imagine how Andrew's future would turn out if, by some chance, Joe won residential custody. I mean, after all, it was possible! Someone did take his case over the phone which told me Joe used his connections to do so. I thought I was up against a battle I may not come up from, and I could potentially lose. Then suddenly, I felt a surge within me. I gained so much strength from within myself. It was almost as if there were a flock of angels surrounding me everywhere, pushing me through and granting me the energy I needed to rise above this battle. So maybe these angels didn't exactly fly per se and maybe they didn't exactly have wings and maybe they weren't all female like in the images we see, but their energy was certainly around me. I was surrounded by all this positive energy or moral souls fighting alongside me!

A thought popped in my head, and it said, *Go and contact and consult with other attorneys, Tania. It's okay! You are not tied to one attorney, and you are allowed to do so. It is your right!* I went ahead and did just that. I researched other attorneys in the area until I found one I felt reputable and credible.

I couldn't believe it! I knew there was someone above on my side! Or was there someone also beside me? I won! Andrew remained in my custody and attended a private Christian school. I was so excited for Andrew to begin his education at a private school. I knew Andrew was worth the money, and I wanted him to have the opportunity to look up to strong men of faith in the community, and I am so grateful he did!

Andrew was grateful to have joined a brotherhood and be schooled by one of the top private schools in the New York area, and I was grateful to support him through it.

Joe's statements made to the court were eventually proven false because they were just that—FALSE. I did enjoy cooking and cleaning, and I was a generous human being. I was a loving soul, and yes, I did live with my family for the short haul. But I was on my way to a phase of healing, and I was going to learn from the mistakes I made in the past. I realized I had found my strength in my mom and support from both my parents. I also found love from my close friends and family members, and I was determined to push through. If my mom could survive a physically and verbally abusive relationship, then I could survive a verbally and emotionally abusive one too. It wasn't long after I realized there was a part of me that relived her very own life. Yes, I won the battle, but I couldn't have done it without all the amazing support and beautiful souls around me. I also couldn't do it without my faith in my God. Above all, I found the greatest love within me and a deeper love for my higher power because of it. I soon felt as if I became just a little closer to my God and once again, my faith was strengthened even more.

I was glad Andrew decided on a private Christian school. I think he, too, realized that we had a choice in life. We could live with God or without him. I think we both knew life was much better with Christ in our lives! Andrew immediately felt at home on the first day of school, and I was so glad he did. I was kinda surprised when he told me he would join track and field then my past popped up again. I enjoyed track in my early years and my dad was a HUGE track star. My uncle spoke about how he and my dad traveled by boat to make competitions all over Eastern Europe. In fact, I still own a picture passed down from my uncle of my dad and his brothers boating across the Baltic Sea. Word spoken was that my dad was a star, and sometimes unstoppable and unbeatable! My brother still tells stories about my dad's athletic abilities. Every now and then, I glance at that picture of my dad. I could take one look and melt at my dad's squinty eyes. I don't know if it is because I feel some form of connection or some kind of deeper understanding of my dad that my siblings or mom could not. I started to see more and more of my Andrew in my father's eyes. Andrew also became a star, and he was in it to win. Andrew told me he enjoyed the feeling of winning against others and that gave him something to feel good about. I quickly realized Andrew was just as competitive as my dad and me.

I didn't realize I was such a contender until my position in business development. I won the sales contest for highest sales in the shortest amount of time! I was on fire, and Andrew followed my very own footsteps! I only slowed when I was struck by another vehicle. It was as if it were a sign, but I was forced to slow down. There was something else waiting for me to finish or to begin, or was it to create? Maybe there was some reason behind this fight and maybe it required me to believe in something other than the well-being of myself. There I went once again...

I was back on the road once again, and I felt all alone. Could anyone really ever fully understand me or my story? It felt so helpless. I felt helpless, and I felt tired of defending myself and all I believed in. Still, I knew I had to keep moving forward because moving backward wasn't an option. I realized it was okay for me to fall, but I had to pick myself back up again because no one was gonna do it for me. My life was ultimately my responsibility, and no one had the power to live it for me. Only I could write my story, and only I was solely responsible for the end of my story. I thought about my life and where I lacked. I had so much love from my family, but I was still lacking in the relationship department and also in my career. What did I really want to be when I grew up? I still wasn't 100 percent sure, but I was sure I absolutely loved being a mom. I was totally sure I was intrigued by the business world, and I was certain I enjoyed helping others. But there was more to me, and I had to find it out. I guess that was when I realized the true meaning behind that old saying, "You must find yourself and conquer self-fulfillment before you could share yourself with a life partner." I became more accomplished in my work life even though I felt as if so much more was to come and be accomplished. Although my search system didn't quite take off as I hoped, it was still a form of my creativity and expression, and it made me feel more confident about my capabilities.

My love life was still absent, and my true soulmate was nowhere to be found. I thought once you found love within yourself was when TRUE ROMANTIC LOVE would appear? I couldn't even envision the image of what my soulmate looked like or was supposed to look like, but I prayed that love would someday be formed, and I envisioned two red hearts intertwined and locked together. The hearts were solid and unbreakable, and they couldn't be cracked or broken. There was no key to open for anyone to enter or intrude upon. It was a love beyond powerful, and it was beautiful, but it didn't exist, or at least, it didn't exist just yet. How would I find it in this modern world we lived in? Was I supposed to be patient and let it stumble upon me in a very natural form or was I supposed to be a little more aggressive and attempt to seek it? After all, the last time was an epic failure when I rolled with it and let love find me. I thought maybe I should have a little more control over who my soulmate would be, so I began to toss around the idea of online dating but I was afraid… still. I knew I had scars from my past. I knew my scars were not visible to those around me and I knew that only I could feel them so I continued to sing.

Because of You

I will not make the same mistake
    that you did
I will not let myself
'Cause my heart so much misery
I will not break the way you did
You fell so hard
I've learned the hard way
To never let it get that far

Because of you
I never stray too far from the
    sidewalk
Because of you
I learned to play on the safe side
    so I don't get hurt
Because of you

I find it hard to trust not only me
　　but everyone around me
Because of you
I am afraid

I was afraid of everyone around me, so how could I possibly be successful in a relationship? I wanted to be like other successful partners so I asked myself, *Where do I begin?* Did we really live in this world where we would be matched up online? Yes, we did, and there were many success stories people spoke about. I guess I had to be open to the idea if I was going to attempt to let love in. But I had fears, so where does a fearful woman begin once again?

As I began to heal, I thought it might be a good idea to at least be social online. I was soon bombarded with messages and offers to chat with men all over the New York area and the bordering tristate area! I became so quickly overwhelmed, and I didn't know where to start. I found the more normal or professional the male was, the further I distanced myself. I was more comfortable speaking to men that didn't seem so perfect or together. I think it was because my life was far from perfect and I had so much further to climb. I found to be more comfortable with people who weren't so conservative because I wasn't. I found myself more comfortable with the quirky or eccentric-type personality, and I wasn't sure how a stranger would feel if I told him I was living with my parents for the time being. There were so many women who had their own apartment or even home, and here I was at my parents with a few investment properties rented out. Would anyone seriously believe me? How would I be able to host at my parents' when there was no extra space? Obviously, I knew I couldn't get too serious at this point in life, but maybe I could find some company to keep? Unfortunately, I had a bad experience and found out the guy I met twice somehow attached his email to my send-out email lists. Not sure what his motive was other than to possibly receive all my online match messages? I was so disgusted. How could someone I barely know invade my life and attempt to control my incoming or outgoing messages? I was in such shock that I actually had to take a screenshot of his email attached to mine which was being forwarded on to. I never mentioned a word to this man, but I was so annoyed that I believe I blocked his number from my incoming calls, and we never spoke again. I was in the middle of a custody battle, and it was awful to find some stranger may have gotten his hands on my personal business.

I took a call from my lawyer outside my office the next day to discuss the motion filed for residential custody. I was relieved to know that there was no way Joe was going to win residential custody, but something had to give because Joe decided to spend thousands on an attorney to represent him. I was granted the same amount of child support for Andrew, but I was responsible to insure Andrew on my policy and Joe be responsible to contribute monthly. I knew that Joe was never going to ACTUALLY contribute to Andrew's medical insurance, but I went ahead with what the attorney suggested. Joe never did offer or send a payment to Andrew's medical insurance, and honestly, could care less whether or not he was insured. I was ultimately responsible for obtaining and managing Andrew's medical costs. Joe never followed any orders for that matter, so I wasn't sure why they even existed? The courts never enforced it, and if I wanted to make an attempt to enforce it, it would cost me money. In any event, I was relieved to know that Andrew would remain under my custody, and Joe didn't have a chance.

As I looked up a moment while speaking to the attorney, I thought I saw a familiar face. The man walked by me rather quickly, and he was dressed in a baseball cap and loungewear. As the man walked by me, he said hello. I responded with hello back, but it wasn't until after he walked out of the building when I realized he looked like someone I knew from the past. Later that evening, I figured out the man looked like Derik, but was it really him? Derik did work in the vicinity, but if it was him, why didn't he stop and chat for a few minutes? I may have been mistaken, but I often wondered if by some chance we crossed paths again.

The final order was received, and Joe lost the case. For the first time in my life, I finally started to understand personality disorders and the characteristics associated with them. I was able to take the information I read online and through softcover books and relate it to my current experiences. It was only because of my readings that I was able to sleep better. I couldn't comprehend how someone could take these extreme measures and master manipulating others around him only to get what he wanted without taking others' feelings or consideration into account. How could someone make a two-page written statement about me that was 90 percent false and react in rage? That was just it, and it was part of a manipulation tactic. In psychology, the term used is projecting due to a lack of self-esteem. Some people use projection as a way to relieve their unwanted feelings and thoughts about themselves. These feelings are pushed onto others in projection.

I felt responsible for Andrew's mental, physical, and emotional health. I had to save him, and I would go to any measure to do so, but it couldn't be possible without believing in myself. I became all I was because of my faith and the power within me that God granted me. I wouldn't have come this far without the strength I had through God, and I would be forever grateful here on. In turn, I had to give back to the Lord for the gifts I received and intake any pain inflicted upon me. I decided that I wasn't making any more deals with the devil. In fact, I wasn't even dancing with the devil. The devil was so distant from me because I had become so close to God. I made a promise to God and that was to continue to walk in his path and follow his footsteps the way he would want us all to do. I made a promise to live in the most moral fashion possible. I realized that no matter where my career path took me, ultimately, I worked for the Lord, and it ultimately came down to right versus wrong and good energy versus bad or evil energy. I would spread my wings wherever I wound up and fight against evil. That meant to conduct every day of my life with a higher obligation to the Lord through honesty to myself and others, kindness, and understanding. I would help those in need, and instill hope in this life and the life after. I would teach our children forgiveness and love the same way our Lord does every day. I stood for respecting others and their space when needed. I didn't believe in prying into others' business, only to envy or desire what they have. I thought about the Ten Commandments and wondered why there was no modern version or detailed explanation as to how we were expected to live our lives in God's name. I found the greatest love of all within myself by the power of God!

I thought of Joe and how these commandments were completely disregarded in his life and how he lived almost in opposition instead of accordingly. Therapists have a tendency to title these character traits as mentally ill, but religion has a tendency to title these traits as evil or ungodly. No matter how you slice it, dice it, or title it, the underlying behavior is immoral, which ultimately leads us back to our Lord in the highest power. I finally understood we had to overcome evil by doing good. I had been at war with evil the past fifteen years. I may have lost a few battles but I felt I was on to win the war and I sang this song...

The Devil Went Down to Georgia
by Charlie Daniels Band

The devil went down to Georgia
He was looking for a soul to steal
He was in a bind 'cause he was
way behind.
He was willing to make a deal
When he came across this young
man sawin' on his fiddle and
playin' it hot
And the devil jumped upon a
hickory stump and said "Boy,
let me tell you what."

"I bet you didn't know it but I'm
a fiddle player, too.
And if you'd care to take a dare
I'll make a bet with you
Now you play a pretty good fiddle, boy, but give the devil his
due
I'll bet a fiddle of gold against
your soul 'cause I think I'm
better than you."

The boy said, "My names Johnny
and it might be a sin, but I'll
take your bet
And you're gonna regret 'cause
I'm the best there's ever been."

Johnny, rosin up your bow and
  play your fiddle hard.
'Cause hell's broke loose in
  Georgia and the devil deals
  the cards.
And if you win you get this shiny
  fiddle made of gold,
But if you lose, the devil gets
  your soul.

The devil opened up case and he
  said, "I'll start this show."
And fire flew from his fingertips
  as he rosined up his bow.
And he pulled the bow across the
  strings and it made an evil hiss
And a band of demons joined in
  and it sounded something like
  this.

When the devil finished, Johnny
  said,
"Well your pretty good ol' son
But sit down in that chair right
  there and let me show you
  how it's done."

"Fire on the mountain." Run,
  boys run!
The devil's in the house of the
  rising sun

Chicken's in the bread pan pick-
  ing out dough
Granny, does your dog bite? No,
  child, no"

The devil's bowed his head
  because he knew that he'd
  been beat
And he laid that golden fiddle on
  the ground at Johnnie's feet
Johnny said, "Devil, just come
  back if you ever wanna try
  again,
'Cause I told you once, you son
  of a bitch—I'm the best there's
  ever been."
And he played
"Fire on the mountain, Run,
  boys, run!
The devil's in the house of the
  rising sun
Chicken's in the bread pan pick-
  ing out dough
Granny, does your dog bite? No,
  child, no"

Chapter 9

The Secret Crush

Andrew remained under my residential custody, and I thanked our dear Lord he did. There was a God, and his angels surrounded me! I began a new chapter in my career as a member of the HR/finance department for a small organization. I was one of two final candidates for the position, but I happened to make the cut. Initially, I interviewed with my manager and then I met with the CFO and finally the VP or soon-to-be president and owner of the company. I was later told that the owner wanted someone with medical experience so that's why I had an edge over the other candidate. It was initially agreed upon with the hiring manager who brought me in that I would start as a payroll associate but quickly have the opportunity to advance within the growing organization. I was soon asked to take on huge tasks such as system data transfers with employee records with very little supervision. I also had to follow through with multiple demands and requests by the manager in order to resolve employee relations issues. Alongside, I was responsible for running the main company payroll including monthly and bonus payments in the HRIS system. I had to run reports for upload into vendor sites after every payroll and conduct audits as needed. Once the system was up and fully running, I had to manage the entire HRIS system, including employee records, time, and data reporting. Employees were often faced with technical difficulties, so I had to manage and resolve the technical difficulties. The new system was fragmented, and there was no real training in order to conduct this job. I was determined to succeed especially since it seemed I was set up to fail. I was told we grew at such a rapid rate and the business office had to catch up. My boss exposed me to all the functions within the finance department, but she wanted me to focus on payroll since she found my strengths in organization and attention to detail.

My performance review was due, and I was shocked not to have received the highest score across the board. During our meeting, my boss came flat out and asked me if I wanted her job. I told my boss that I wanted to advance, but we could advance together. There was no need for anyone to so call "TAKE" anyone's job. I was SHOCKED and totally taken off guard. I realized my boss was totally threatened about her job, but she was awesome at it, and there was no reason at all for her to feel that way. I was truly disheartened, and it was disappointing that after all I did and the good examples I set, my boss still carried these fears. Still, I had a job to perform and life carried on. Everything and anything I was asked to do was completed by the deadline. The employees looked to me for guidance and assistance; and the owner's son, Ian, commented that I was one of the best employees he ever had. I was never late, nor was I ever written up. My work was second to none, and I was unstoppable considering the tools I had to support me.

My schedule was supposed to consist of 37.5 hours a week, but there was too much work in my department, so I started my date at 8:30 a.m., skipped lunch, and ended about five-ish. I took it all in stride because I had an appetite to learn as much as I could and the will to achieve. The owner would ask me for assistance every now and then, and I was very receptive to his business needs. There wasn't a manager in the company who could honestly say I was not very helpful or resourceful except for possibly one employee in the finance department. I was dedicated and committed to my work, and I stood for fairness and righteousness in the workplace. I knew what it was like to be treated unfairly, and I worked as hard as I could for the protection of the employees and the company. I used my best judgment when working with employee relations and never operated based on emotions. I interpreted company policy and upheld both federal and state laws and regulations. I stayed completely true to myself, and I was promoted after eight months of my employment. I was soon offered a recruiting manager role, but it consisted of travel, and I felt too connected and needed in the office. I could be more resourceful working with operations and finance. Besides, someone had to run payroll! We were an operation without a payroll company growing so rapidly with 150 employees.

So why did my manager not rate my performance properly? After all, she was supposed to stand for fairness and act accordingly to her own company policies she created. My manager was placed in a position of power to follow through her role in the HR department as a leader to inspire and serve as a role model. I started to notice odd behavior by my manager and although she said I had to earn my money, it almost seemed an excuse for her bully behavior. Although my manager gave me an average rating score, I was promoted with a raise after I wrote down a long list of duties that I was now solely responsible for. My manager was not always chipper with me, but she bought me flowers, chocolates, and muffins for my birthday; so underneath all that madness, I must have been appreciated on some level! My manager said she was so grateful to have met me, and she was truly appreciative of all my hard work. The boss felt I truly deserved my raise, and I would amount to be quite some HR manager someday.

After my promotion, the behavior seemed to become almost malicious as she turned against me. I noticed the work was not diverted fairly, and I was overwhelmed with most of the HR responsibility. All of the leaders' requests were directed to me, including the owner's, amongst all my other work. In other words, my manager's work was now being directed to me while she shopped online and planned party functions on a PT basis. I needed an assistant, but she hired a recruiting manager to relieve her of even more functions and responsibilities.

I walked past the elevator to get to the stairway when I spotted this handsome, striking mail carrier. Whew! How could anyone help but notice this powerful presence? This carrier didn't appear to be your ordinary mail carrier, and he was in our building, but what was he doing? Did someone call security? I proceeded toward the elevator when I heard a deep voice from the corner side of me ask, "Are you going up?"

I responded in a very coy manner, "No, I am fine, but thank you."

I opted for the staircase up to the second floor, and I remembered he was the same guy I spotted in the window when he pulled his truck close up to my window. I couldn't believe how tall this man was, probably about 6'3" and 230 pounds, with a shape like a Chippendale on a calendar or a National Guard.

I said aloud, "Wow! He must work out!" I have never seen anyone with that kind of appearance in the workplace, and it was totally eye-catching and distracting. These kinds of physiques were not normally spotted in office buildings!

Odd days came up when I was asked if I spoke to the owner's son out of the clear blue. I started to feel so self-conscious of my relationship with the owner's son, Ian, and I thought my boss may be telling me something. Was Ian upset with me because I didn't speak to him too often? I didn't want to upset anyone at work especially the son of the owner of the company.

The next day, I made a point to stop in Ian's office to ask how things were going. Ian said he was okay, and he heard that I was doing awesome and kick-ass work. I told him that I was sorry if I wasn't too attentive or social with him lately but I was overwhelmed with work. I tried to keep the social contact to a minimum with everyone so I could maintain a professional demeanor. I also let Ian know that if he needed anything at all just to let me know. Ian smiled, turned coy while he blushed, and said he would do. We left off in a very professional manner, and I felt somewhat relieved. Ian wasn't the easiest person to engage in a social conversation, but at least, I can say I tried. Every time I tried to engage in some conversation, I felt awkward because it was uncomfortable. It almost felt like there was something deep and hidden unbeknownst to the rest.

I noticed my boss became a block for me to communicate with Ian for her personal gain or protection. I can even remember, one day, watching my boss walk to Ian's office and pace back and forth for his attention to avoid any contact between him and me. It was very odd, and I couldn't figure out if my boss truly had a crush on Ian or if she was just fearful of her job and intimated by my performance. Either way, I noticed envious emotions and bitter words, and it didn't make me feel very comfortable.

I couldn't believe one sunny morning when my boss happened to be in her office earlier than expected. After I walked in and settled at my office, she yelled out, "Tania?"

I responded with, "Yes!"

She said, "Why are we led to believe blonds are dumb?"

The comment was directed to me in a very sarcastic manner. I truly had enough of the bully treatment by now, but I held my own. I responded with, "Not really sure! I do believe some people are quick to judge and may tend to believe that blondes are not that bright until that one just happens to surprise you."

I think my boss almost choked. She knew I was on to her, and I figured out she hired me because she thought I was dumb, and when she found out I wasn't, I guess it ruined her plan. That made a lot of sense why she hired a recruiter with no real experience at a salary higher than mine. Another blonde, by the way—I was shocked! That day confirmed my boss was not supportive of my work, and she was actually out to sabotage me. Why would someone turn on me to that level for no reason? There had to be more behind this story...

My boss was terminated about a week later, and although I was not shocked, I was a little upset. I recall my boss's last words over a conversation in our office were about the owner. My boss stated it very clear that he was a PUSSY and didn't have the balls to confront people or ask them on a date. The new recruiter and I were in the office, and we both looked at each other in awe. The recruiter and I were brought into the conference room by the compliance officer the next day or so to be informed our boss was no longer with the company. The recruiter wondered if there was a voice recorder in our office. I swore IT built it into the computer speaker. Rumor was the boss was terminated for charging personal items on her company credit card. I believe it was a cover-up, and the real reason was that she began to block my communications with the owner's son.

The owners immediately brought in an SVP of human resources about a week later, and we were told we were now on a corporate level and need someone to take on a high-level HR role. At that time, I respected the decision, but I believed it was to justify the termination of my boss and dodge a lawsuit. After all, my boss did shop often, but she was not given a budget and no one stopped her before. The boss said she confused her personal Amex with her corporate once before, but it never seemed to be a major issue with the founder of the company after she just reimbursed him. The boss was careless at times, but she knew it was a weakness of hers. Overall, she was a hands-on manager, which most of the employees came to miss. I found it extremely odd that since I had completely run the HR department alongside my manager that I wouldn't have any input in what was needed within the department or the next step. There was no communication for the interim on the plans for the HR department, and I was left to run

HR business as usual. I prepared and ran three pay-rolls in my position along with all the other day-to-day operations in the department besides recruiting.

Ian was very involved with my work duties and gave me the final approval on submissions to the third-party vendors. If Ian was not in a great mood, I would receive a one-word response or no response. If Ian was in a decent mood, I would receive a smi-ley face and even a "Hello" or "How are you?" The controller in finance seemed to be the middle man with a close connection to Ian and a gateway into my workday. Ian would drum up unnecessary com-plaints with the controller so it would refer back to me, and I just to cause havoc in my day.

One of the long-standing employees just so happened to stop in my office and ask to speak to me, but I could tell she felt somewhat awkward. This conversation was not over a personal issue of hers, but rather, involved me. When I asked what was up, this employee came right out to ask what my relationship status was. I asked why and she said, "Someone has been asking around about you and he would like to get to know you."

I thought, *OH NO! WHOOO COULD IT BE?* I didn't want to hear it was the boss! I was nervous to respond, but she said, "He is a really handsome guy and has been working on deliveries for nearly twenty years now." Gia mentioned this gentleman is a Union Laborer and has older children like me and also lives in the area. I told her I would consider it, but I wasn't sure if I wanted to date anyone.

A week passed, and this gentleman asked about me again and said I didn't call. This time, he asked for my phone in case I was shy. Gia thought he was a nice guy and that maybe I should just go out and see where it progressed. I figured out exactly who asked about me and I thought of our elevator encounter. Everyone thought we would make a nice-looking couple. About a week or so later, I caved in and gave this handsome man named Dean a call. I knew we would eventually bump into each other again if I didn't call.

The first day our new SVP of HR began work, she briefly introduced herself and asked if I had any questions for her. My biggest concern was the structure in the department since all the HR duties along with the entire payroll function fell on my lap. The new boss said she had both worked in a structured environment and created it. Something in her facial expression told me she wasn't being very truthful. Only a few days later, the founder popped into our office as he often did at the end of a business day. It happened to be just my boss and me in the department when he asked when his son's last raise was and how much. Following that, he mentioned that his son was a numbers guy and had a profile on me. I wasn't exactly sure what he meant by that so I asked him to explain what he meant by a "profile." Ian's dad said an eye for me.

I said, "Now?" I wanted to tell him that I just started seeing someone because he had the courage to ask me but I just couldn't say that. I really wanted to say that his son confused me by his behavior, but I didn't have the courage to say that, either. I was totally flattered but taken off guard. I knew that dating in the workplace could potentially cause problems, and I was too loyal to my career. I told Ian's dad that I thought Ian would want to settle down with someone a little younger than me.

Ian's dad said, "Well, how old are you?"

When I told Ian's dad my age, he said I didn't look it. I also said I thought Ian was in a serious relationship and I had already started engaging in communication with a handsome Dean. In fact, Ian JUST brought his girlfriend to the Christmas party and also introduced her to me in the office so how could he be interested in me? I also mentioned that I, through his son, would want a big family; and well… I already had a son soon to be off to college. I asked how things were working out with his girlfriend, and he said that he didn't want to marry her. Now I thought that was awful to say because Ian was in a serious relationship that he wasn't totally devoted to and now he wanted to engage in something with me when I already started a relationship with Dean?

My boss quickly cut off Ian's dad and commented that she was surprised he would say that to me when he walked out of our office. I told my boss that I was totally confused and wouldn't feel so comfortable dating or being romantically involved with my employer. I also felt Ian wouldn't have any problems finding his match. In fact, the recruiter's daughter was single, and OH, how we all heard about it.

I maintained my professional relationship with the leadership team and continued my job. The founder of the company said he retired, and Ian completely ghosted after he stepped down as president of the company to board member. Our department was moved from the lower-level quarters to the second-floor executive level. HR was tucked away in a cornered section with an automated lock so no employees could enter without one of us allowing entry. I assumed the main reason for the move was to keep the mail carrier out of my office since he had easy access to the lower level. I felt my decision wasn't respected, and this was an act of retaliation in the workplace.

Our new SVP of HR, Kate, began showing up at odd hours and was totally uninvolved with HR department operations. Then Kate began to make up excuse after excuse such as she hit her head or fell on the ice or had a dental appointment. I also heard Kate would not be available since she had to care for her mom or daughter at a doctor's appointment. I couldn't believe how someone could just begin employment and be totally absent and be accepted by the top leadership team. It was unheard of before with any other employee, and I was in complete shock!

The AVP to the finance team and the executive assistant to the owner were on a complete rampage and took it to another level. They started tracking the SVP of HR's time as well as her performance or lack thereof. They knocked on my door often to ask where my boss was and where she disappeared to. I had no idea where the boss would disappear to, but she often arrived at the office around 10:00 a.m. to 11:00 a.m.

I noticed my boss pull up to the lot the same time as Dean did and literally eyed him from head to toe, but how did she know he and I were friends and why did want to check him out? I also noticed Kate had disappeared in the afternoon where she could not be found until she returned several hours later to finally leave before me. When I asked the executive assistant to the owner what she was hired to do, she replied the same job as my previous manager. My response was that she didn't take on any duties in HR, so that left me with all the work responsibilities.

Employees were enraged and began to send emails to the new SVP as well as the founder in question how someone could get away with such a lack of response to the employees' needs but operate and even lead the resource department. It was completely contradictory. When I finally asked my boss how she could not have any experience with payroll, her response was that she was not hired to perform that function. I explained that my previous boss did perform that function, so I wanted clarification that it was now ultimately my responsibility without any other assistance. I was completely swamped with work and more confused than ever. Anytime I sent an email out to the new boss, I didn't receive a response or it was completely delayed and only acknowledged if I was able to catch her in her office.

Not one meeting was called in several months to direct the HR Team or support us until the recruiter and I questioned Kate's leadership and spoke about it several times in the office. When our leader finally did schedule a meeting, there was no solid plan for direction or function within the department. The meeting was quickly turned over to us as if we were supposed to lead the meeting.

Our boss seemed to have a close connection with operations of sales, but she carried a very nonchalant and uncaring attitude about the HR department operations. The recruiter would send out offer letters with errors that were not corrected and the job descriptions were not completed. There was no real solid background check for the candidates, and the recruiter had no idea how to document I-9 verifications or interpret the handbook. I was somewhat frustrated that she was paid more than me, but I had to train her. There was no one managing the recruiter, and she needed guidance in her work. When the recruiter and I finally had enough and wanted answers, we had a conversation with our leader's boss. The compliance officer was recently promoted to CEO, and he was also nonchalant and not very responsive. The recruiter thought he was protecting our boss since he brought her into the company and said we probably wouldn't get very far with him. Some employees even questioned whether or not there was a romantic relationship between the two since nothing else made sense for this performance. The pressure was bestowed upon me, and employees wanted answers! Employee managers needed direction, but the new HR leader was not responsive for several months now. Finally, the AVP of finance said it had to stop and someone had to speak with the owners. I was asked to have a conversation with both owners so they were fully aware of the fact that my boss was not conducting her job. I agreed to meet with the owners or Ian in hopes of some improvement.

The executive assistant to Ian arranged a meeting with me for 6:00 p.m., after hours. Ian's assistant said he did want the new CEO or my boss to find out about the meeting. I was totally confused by that statement, but I agreed to meet anyway. Six in the evening came around, and the owners were nowhere in sight. Ian's assistant called my office line to let me know the owners were in traffic and would be running behind. The assistant to Ian also asked if Ian could phone me back with an ETA. I recently changed my personal cell, and I wasn't comfortable with anyone knowing my cell so I informed Ian's assistant that she or he could call me on my office line as I would wait. I had a feeling that the owners wanted to get their hands on my personal cell for their personal benefits, and I was no longer comfortable with them knowing too much of my personal life.

The owners finally arrived an hour later, and we had a discussion in Ian's office. I presented the facts about the working environment and notes I had taken. I mentioned that employees were very upset at the lack of communication and I needed support.

When I asked how my boss could arrive at her job at 11:00 a.m. when there was so much work to be done in the office, he responded by stating she could be working from home.

Ian's dad said, "Just because she isn't present in the office does not mean she is not working."

I was totally lost since I thought my boss was hired to support the HR department, and I also explained the recruiter needed direction. I further went on to explain that payroll was a main function, and I needed support. Instead of offering an assistant to me, Ian's dad mentioned they were working on that and seeking a new hire. Ian's dad said they were seeking to find the right person to take over the entire payroll function. I explained that would work, too, as long as I was guided or supported in another role. Shortly after, I recall my boss told me otherwise and said she was seeking a payroll associate or support. Once again, I was completely confused and insecure about my position. Ian seemed very calm throughout the entire meeting, but his dad seemed somewhat thrown off or perturbed. I was actually surprised Ian's dad showed up to the meeting since he was so-called retired.

Months passed and still, it seemed as though our new leader, Kate was completely uninvolved in the HR duties. I did notice my boss and the founder shared a lot of communications together, especially for someone who just so-called retired. Days carried on, but the work was never quite divided up fairly, and I thought it may have been on purpose to make me quit. There were meetings taking place between the new CEO and HR leader, but they were behind closed doors and the HR team was not included. Most people would not be able to work under those conditions, but I hung tight because I relied on my career. Ian barely spoke to me when he showed up to work, which was on rare occasions. Ian stepped down as president and his title changed to board member, which was when I realized he had a secret crush on me. I mentioned that I couldn't date my employer or owner of the company I worked for due to the potential abuse of power if the relationship went sour. I had an obligation as an HR leader to protect the company and the owners vested. I also had the obligation to protect myself as an employee from any abuse, hostility, sexual harassment in the workplace. We were all safer by me dating the handsome mail carrier, but some people just couldn't and wouldn't accept that. I thought in rational terms, and I cared for the owner's family I worked for, but I guess, the family I worked for didn't see that.

Chapter 10

An Imperfect Love

I didn't initially realize I was being LOVE-BOMBED! I thought about when Dean and I first met, and I glanced at the tiny note handed to me with perfect handwriting that read, "Dean," with his phone attached. I thought I would at least introduce myself and see where the call would lead us.

When Dean picked up the phone, I said, "Hello! I heard you were asking around about me."

Dean laughed and said he was asking about me, as a matter a fact. We spoke about fitness and spirituality. I was completely honest about my current status, and I could sense that Dean felt sincere appreciation for me being just that.

We initially hit it off and agreed to a cocktail at some point. It was an instant connection; and our words, values, and ideas just flowed. Several days later, I lost my contact list because my phone fell in my cup of coffee. Dean didn't reach out to me, either, and it had to be about two weeks later when I told Gia what happened so Dean wouldn't feel so bad. I felt so terrible that this handsome man had enough courage to ask someone he barely knew to call him and I failed. I hoped Dean would be super understanding as I was undergoing a lot of pressure at work and subjected to constant secretive behavior.

After Dean found out what happened, he reached out to me again, and we finally went out for a drink. We had a nice conversation and two drinks each. My drink was lit up in a flame with a rosemary stem and a lemon twist. Dean looked stark and handsome that evening, dressed in a black fitted high-neck sweater. I noticed he was super fit with large hands and a manly touch. After a nice conversation, I was ready to call it an evening, but Dean asked that I pop in his car for a quick good night chat. I wasn't particularly interested in fast sports cars or big muscle men so I wasn't sure if Dean was truly my type. I was taken back at how soon Dean was interested in a romantic kiss. I told him that I wasn't quite ready for that, but I knew where the relationship was headed. There was a physical attraction, and I think it had to do with the heart I saw deep within. Valentine's Day came around, and Dean was determined to sneak a rose into my office. Employee personnel could not get in my office so they told him to try again later when I arrived at my desk.

I happened to be at the gym when I received a call from Dean requesting that I meet him at the local bar since he was in the area visiting a family member. How could I say no? I made it out to say hello, and

I immediately felt an attraction again. It was as if I was the most important person in the world to Dean at that moment and was serious about a relationship. Dean asked to walk me home, and I wasn't planning on inviting him in until he asked to see my home and how I lived. It was as if Dean already knew how organized and clean I maintained my professional and personal life order. We turned on the TV and after a few brief words were spoken, Dean leaned in to kiss me. We shared our first kiss, and it was so passionate. I couldn't believe how soft and seductive. It felt as if we were in love forever! It was the first time I truly enjoyed kissing for a long period. It was the longest kiss I EVER FELT! I wasn't sure what got over me because I enjoyed the kiss so much that I didn't want to stop. It was in the kiss that told me there was a major physical attraction or combustion! We kissed the entire evening for hours, and well, didn't make out much of the movie.

> Oh What a Night
> Elvis
>
> It was a night oo-oo what a night
> It was it really was such a night
> The moon was bright on how so
>   bright
> It was it really was such a night
> The night was alight with stars
>   above

Oo-oo when she kissed me
I had to fall in love

Oh it was a kiss oo-oo what a kiss
It was it really was such a kiss
Oh how she could kiss oh what
    a kiss
It was it really was such a kiss
Just the thought of her lips
Sets me afire
I reminisce and I'm filled with
    desire
But I'd gave my heart to her in
    sweet surrender
How well I remember, I'll always
    remember

Oh what a night oo-oo what a
    night
It was it really was such a night
Came the dawn and my heart
    and her love
And the night was gone
But I'll never forget the kiss
The kiss in the moonlight
Oo-oo such a kiss, such a nigh

It was a night...

We both had to report to work the next morning, but we were exhausted from all that kissing!

The next morning, my eyes felt drained and my energy was diminished, but all I could think of what that amazing feeling Dean and I felt the night before from that kiss! Oh my gosh! He just pulled up to my window, and he looked more handsome than before! Dean popped into my office to say a quick hello and said I looked so beautiful even as tired as I was. I could tell Dean's face turned to color when he looked at me, and my whole body wanted to melt right there in his arms, but we were in the office! We gave each other a warm hug and left each other with a beautiful smile. I couldn't wait to spend more time outside of work with Dean again! Word spread quickly, and everyone knew how deeply I was admired by this handsome man and the feelings were mutual.

Soon after, I noticed more cameras displayed in every entranceway and office, so I asked Dean to respect my space in the professional office so I wasn't the center of attention. Employees started to behave differently and the work environment turned strange. Some employees stopped talking to me as often, and I assume it was as a result of intimidation by Dean. Others seemed overly nosy and would wait by the door or the lab just to get a glimpse of handsome Dean. In fact, our CEO even walked upstairs to the third level to eye Dean up and down. The recruiter would arrive at work same time as Dean and attempt to ride the elevator with him. I couldn't believe the distracted behavior that I was surrounded by. Very few seemed happy for us, but the few that were did not suffer from any jealousy or envy issue. As our relationship grew, so did the tension. Ian completely ghosted and didn't show up for work at all! Ian's dad stopped visiting me in my office when he stopped in the building.

My work became more difficult due to technical difficulties and the support from our leaders was nonexistent. Since I was left with all the admin duties in the department, I thought it might behoove me to learn as much as I could, so I signed up for a management course. When I asked for the reimbursement, I was given a complete run around by the owners and CEO. Everyone seemed to be paid at a generous salary with large bonuses that I had to enter in payroll, except me. When my performance review was due, I was ignored once again. I felt like I was the only employee totally excluded. I noticed unpleasant looks through the glass window, and I felt as if the leaders were in discussion about me behind my back all too often. Kate would pop in around my desk area, unannounced, very often to see what I was working on. I found it quite odd that she never visited the recruiter across me to see what she was working on but was somehow overly concerned about what was displayed on my computer screen. Since I was an honest and loyal worker, Kate struggled to catch me in the act, but she often tried. I couldn't believe the treatment I was subjected to by supposed to be intelligent business leaders all because of my personal business.

Dean would ask how my day was, and I would explain in hopes of his support but it only aggravated him and he became irate. We tried to live as a happy couple in the dating phase, but it became very difficult. We were in agreement to see each other once during the week and every weekend. Sometimes, Dean asked that I meet him outside work or invite him in for a quick visit, but I didn't always feel so comfortable when I agreed to do so. I became so sick from the tension and developed a ring of cold sores around my lips. Dean was sweet enough to drop off homemade soup in my car at work and wanted to spend time anyway. Along with homemade chicken soup were a piece of bread, a wedge of lemon, and a love note that read, "Feel better, baby." I realized Dean did truly care about me, and it made me more even more attracted to him. I visited Dean at his apartment late that Saturday after my cousin left from working on my house. We shared great conversation, and I felt Dean was a true gentleman who seemed happy to serve me. We had engaged in the longest conversation together for hours, and I was comforted to know we had more than just a physical attraction and there was a strong mental connection as well.

In the beginning, Dean seemed patient and understanding but a few months into the relationship, his behavior started to change. Was it because he was in fear of losing me or was it because he had his own issues within that were unresolved? After all, no one is perfect, and it is our own expectations that disappoint us. I later learned that it may have been both fear and past issues that caused both Dean and I to feel unsettled in our relationship. My fear brought me back to a similar place in time.

It was St. Patrick's Day and I was totally excited to visit a local bar with Dean and enjoy a traditional St. Pat's day out. I had been in a very lively and joyous mood. I felt like I was on top of the world. I could express my personality with a bodyguard behind me. I finally felt somewhat FREE from my chains tied to Joe. I met many people that evening and even walked over to the band and sang a Bruce Springsteen song with the band! We even drank a few shots, and our energy was elevated. The music turned loud and the crowd was overwhelming, so we couldn't carry on an intimate conversation.

Dean seemed content guarding us that evening and so I sang a song with the band. I thought Dean enjoyed his time, too, but maybe not as much as I did. We went out the following week to a different local bar and the energy was a bit more low-key. People seemed to approach us, and I think it was as a result of how large Dean's physique was. The couple next to us struck up a conversation, and I was completely engaged. I considered myself a social being and thought nothing wrong of it while I was getting to know Mr. Dean. That evening, I saw another side to Dean when we returned to my home. I soon found out that Dean wasn't too comfortable with who I was. I was completely shocked when Dean raised his voice at me, completely enraged! I was called disrespectful and flirtatious with strangers including women! I agreed to tone it down for next time, but I disagreed with Dean. Clearly, this was the beginning of a control battle I might lose. I wasn't as attentive to Dean as I could have been, but I wasn't perfect either!

Dean moved pretty quickly and asked that I meet his children very soon. I thought Dean was super serious about our relationship at that point, and I was totally in! We met up at a local restaurant and enjoyed the conversation and time shared. I noticed Dean had his eye on the front door the entire time as if he was top security. I may have had one or two drinks that evening but not enough not to remember the evening. Later that evening, I felt so dizzy that the room started to spin. I didn't remember most of the night, but I do recall we had some form of intimacy. I recalled the sexual demands of Dean, but I was too dizzy to fight it. There was something sexy about sexual submission, and pleasing Dean. I knew Joe would eventually find out about Dean because nothing was private these days with social media. I thought it might intimidate him and force him to live up to his responsibility financially for Andrew. Years flew by without child support and medical insurance was picked up on my behalf for Andrew. It was nice to receive support for Andrew without a legal battle for once.

Dean began to text more often, and he began to demand more attention and time, but I was fighting a hidden battle most didn't know anything about. The texts were mostly very affectionate and loving, but I had to respond quickly or Dean would become agitated and upset. It became tough to manage Dean and all my work drama all at the same time, but I hung in there in hopes to make it all work out. I gave in to the sexual demands until I could no longer manage them. My energy was depleting. I responded to texts as often as I could during work and after, but it didn't seem to be enough attention for Dean. I spent as much time with Dean as I possibly could, but he didn't feel I wanted to be around him enough. Dean never seemed satisfied with what I could give him at that time, and I soon began to feel hopeless. I felt like a disappointment to Dean, and I started to wonder if I was the right partner for Dean. I was told by Dean that he could find someone better than me and he would do so if I didn't change my ways. I was so hurt by those words, but I knew some words were said out of frustration.

We happened to be at a local party when Dean became enraged over living arrangements. Dean and I were in disagreement and an argument broke out. Dean zoomed back to my place and demanded that I open the door so he could grab his belongings to head back home. I informed Dean that he could wait outside, and I would bring out his belongings but he wouldn't budge. A loud argument broke out, and my voice was elevated! Dean sped off after I gave him his bag, and soon after, the police department arrived at my front door and asked if all was okay. I explained that Dean and I had an argument and didn't want to carry it in my home so I demanded that he wait outside. The police officer confirmed it was my home and then shook his head and wished me a good night. The relationship became dysfunctional and unhealthy too soon. I didn't speak to Dean for several weeks nor was I sure we would speak again until we ran into each other on my way to work.

I took one look up out my window, and there he was, behind the wheel of his truck with that loving face. I couldn't help but smile, and I think at that time, Dean's heart wanted to melt because he looked back at me with a half-witted smile. Dean texted me that he still loved me, and I agreed to meet him again because my feelings for him were too strong. Although I was scared the relationship may cause heartbreak, I wanted to try to work out our issues. We discussed our feelings and I admitted that I would try harder, but it seemed difficult for Dean to admit any wrongdoing. I thought I was dealing with pure stubbornness with an authoritative-type personality. I felt I was getting older and failed too many times before in relationships, so I wanted to try super hard to make this one work. I saw a broken man with a heart, and I thought I might be able to fix it with a little patience. I knew Dean came from a broken past but so did I. I believed that people can overcome trauma in childhood because I did, and I was living proof. I assumed our childhood suffering was our major connection and may be the reason our energy connected. We agreed there was still enough love within to attempt to make it work once again.

I drank more than usual, most likely from all the stress I was faced with at work, but I stayed the course. Dean and I spent most weekends together, including

Saturday and Sunday, until I had an annual holiday party to attend. Although it was ladies only, Dean could have also joined me. Dean was not happy to be separated, but I went anyway. I drank more than I should and my girlfriends wanted me to stay over. Dean flipped out when I called him and demanded I drive back home so clearly he wasn't concerned about my safety. My girlfriends were ticked off that I left the party sooner than normal and they were worried about my driving, but Dean didn't have a care in the world about my safety. That told me he was consumed with only himself. I made it home to meet Dean waiting for me at my back door. I continued the party and my drink when I got home. I tried to forget about my problems so I drank and danced the evening night away.

The next morning, I vomited for hours with a severe headache and hangover. Dean lectured me about my drinking and asked if I wanted to continue this behavior at my age. Obviously, I did not want to feel like crap but I had such a large load over my shoulder to carry.

Dean and I decided to take a mini getaway since we were both under a little stress. When I initially requested the time off for my birthday weekend, I was denied by my boss. I made a point to say that no one in the entire company has even been denied paid time off, but I happened to be the exception. When I followed up on the denial with Kate, she said it was as a result of her planned function she already committed to, but I knew it was totally to spite me.

I remained calm and rescheduled my vacation for the following week. Kate had no other option but to approve my time off since it was the second time I requested it, and I had earned and accrued the time off. I just couldn't comprehend how Kate could come and go as she pleased, barely work in the office, take off an enormous amount of PTO but deny mine. It just felt so awful and cruel.

Dean and I had a fabulous long weekend as it was well overdue. We initially arrived at the hotel backing up to a historic train station. Dean and I couldn't keep our hands off each other as we kissed the night away! After Dean and I shared tremendous love followed by passionate sex, we enjoyed a steak dinner. Dean and I were able to walk around a few of the shops and even make a birthday purchase. I found a unique poncho sweater that seemed to suit me well and a trendy crossover with patchwork. We held hands the entire night and kissed all too often. It was rather a chilly evening, but Dean was sure to keep me warm in his bare chest and oversized arms.

The following day, we shared a champagne toast to my birthday and went out to lunch. We walked by a few historic sights and checked out some real estate. It was time to pack up, but Dean will spend the night over at my place back at home. The toughest times were when we had to part the next day because we were more comfortable and at peace within as a couple together. I soon realized all hell broke loose only when we were distant from each other.

Although I was under a lot of stress at work, I made an effort to communicate with Dean at least once a day in the evening by convo or text before bedtime. We always expressed our love for each other, but it was easier when we were together. At times, I sensed fear which turned into anger and devaluation when we were apart.

Dean and I spoke about living together, but I was in no rush. The thought of companionship was comforting, but something didn't quite feel right, and I was in no rush to escalate our relationship to the next level. Dean called me up one evening enraged that I was not excited about living together or the relationship. Dean said we haven't spoken enough about it and made zero plans. I couldn't argue because it was true, and I wasn't 100 percent confident the relationship would work. Many relationships failed, so how would we keep ours alive?

I had to manage caring for Andrew, an unpleasant workplace, a romantic relationship as well as study for my management class test. Technical difficulties continued at work, and the IT department seemed sketchy. One of the IT members would enter a private room across my office at least five times a day and then walk by my office as he glanced my way. I often wondered who managed this department, what the IT's responsibilities were, and who they reported to. It seemed as though they were paid to spy. I do recall a photo of Ian shaking the Top IT leader's hand during his promotion so there must have been a close connection between the two. There were constant distractions, and no one was ever reprimanded. I felt like I worked at the Wild West.

I started to notice paperwork mailed in didn't reach me and faxed documents failed to send over. I recall when the CEO initially came by my office during the early stages of Kate's employment and checked my computer screen to see what I was working on and then abruptly handed me a garnishment and said the paperwork was never mailed in. I never received it, and I informed him I would take care of it ASAP! I often found myself documenting and making copies as a backup of my work just to defend myself from what I felt was a plot and constant attack against me.

Dean and I would discuss work from time and time and compare notes. I would notice a change in the COO's behavior toward me as rather cold one day, and Dean would tell me they met in the elevator and spoke briefly about Dean's long-term employment as a mail carrier. I couldn't believe the time these people at work had on their hands and how much they were paid for it.

Valentine's Day was around the corner, and this year, Dean and I had plans to see *Phantom of the Opera* in the BIG CITY. We drove into Times Square, but because of tremendous traffic, we just made the show! I had never seen the city that crowded; but there were people all over the streets on foot, car, and bike. It seemed as though we were gridlocked, and everything moved in slow motion. We headed toward the show when a driver came from nowhere with a top speed of about sixty down a side street and almost struck me.

Dean yelled, "Tania!" as he towered over me and pushed me toward the sidewalk. My hood on my jacket blocked my peripheral vision, and I didn't see the car driving toward me. Super Dean saved my life, or at least protected me from a possible second spine injury!

The show was phenomenal, and our seats were second-row midsection. We enjoyed a few cocktails and amazing New York pizza following the show. Dean stood close by me and protected me from any stranger with close contact. We had a great time spent alone together, but our weekends always flew by too quickly, and there was never enough time for our relationship!

I looked forward to the weekends as a break away from all the stress at work only to stumble upon more chaos. Dean had joined me at my parents' home on one Sunday afternoon. Dean had welcomed his daughters over as well on what started to be a sunny, beautiful day. We often shared many laughs at our family and friend functions, and this day was no different. I had enjoyed more cocktails than I honestly should have and didn't eat very much. I started to really enjoy myself as the music turned up. I don't think Dean was feeling as happy as I was to enjoy myself. I couldn't understand why anyone would care if I enjoyed myself? Unfortunately, Dean placed my life in extreme danger, and I could have killed myself. Dean demanded that I drive his car back home, but my mom was furious with his demand and behavior. My mom couldn't believe that Dean would make this demand in such a forceful manner.

My mom said, "No, Tania is not driving anyone or any car anywhere. She can't drive! Have you seen her condition, Dean?"

Dean said, "Oh yes, she can, Jana. If she could drive back from her girlfriends' then she could drive my car home."

My mama said, "I cannot believe you are arguing with me right now!"

Dean shouted, "I will be in the car with her so she will be fine!"

I didn't want to cause any problems and I wasn't in any condition to fight so I went along with Dean and drove his car home. Still to this day, I am not sure how I made it home because I don't remember much of that drive home. I thanked the Lord above for another day!

The next day, Dean didn't mention a word about his demand or my condition. My mom called me to tell me that she was not happy with what she observed, and she would call me another time to speak in detail. Later that evening, Dean called me after dinner, and I told him that my mom was very upset and I knew why. I explained to him my mom was upset because of his demands and being forced to drive when I couldn't remember much of the remainder of that evening.

Dean immediately raised his voice at me and said well, my mom shouldn't force alcohol on anyone. Instead of a simple apology, Dean placed blame on my mom. Obviously, Dean wanted to control my alcohol intake that evening, but he didn't act on it in the safest manner. I cut the conversation off and didn't bother making contact that evening or the day after. Dean asked me to leave his belongings in the shed for pick up, and I didn't argue. I determined that I was in a toxic relationship that would never benefit me. Although I was completely heartbroken, I knew I had to keep my distance before matters worsened. I felt I had so many excellent qualities, but I was confused why the relationship failed. I felt less worthy and like a failure. I started researching personality and to my surprise, I found I had *Empath traits*.

Chapter 11

Love by an Empath

I was back in the single life. I confirmed I was the empath when I recalled a time I had shopped for my pet in the pet store. I was in a long line with an angry customer in front of me. The cashier was fairly young, with pretty blonde hair, and she seemed to be new and probably in training. Although the cashier seemed so pleasant, she was a little confused. The angry customer raised her voice with a demeaning comment directed at the cashier which quickly upset her. I heard the customer say, "Why didn't you tell me that before I waited in this long line?"

The cashier broke down in tears as the customer walked away. It was my turn to be waited on, and I felt so sad for the cashier. I wanted to comfort her with a hug, but I didn't even have a tissue to hand her. I told the cashier not to take the comments to heart and ruin her day. I explained people can be rude and unhappy within so they direct their frustrations at others. The cashier wiped her tears with her sleeve, nodded her head, and gasped for a breath of air as she rang me up. When I opened my car door and sat behind the wheel of my car, I broke down in tears. I felt so hurt that I couldn't even begin to drive so I stayed parking for a few minutes until the pain disappeared. I wasn't sure exactly what was happening to me, but my stomach felt like sharp knives were jabbed into it. It was at that very moment when I realized that I felt that cashier's pain, and there had to be some spiritual reason for it. The only logical reason I felt that way was to take her pain away or relieve her from the hurt.

I woke up the next morning and dressed for a new day at work! I pulled into the lot and parked my vehicle rather close to corporate's back door. I proceeded to exit my car when Dean's truck pulled into the lot rather aggressively. It didn't take me long to realize it was him! Oh my GOSH! I took a glance behind me and thought to myself, *This is way too early for small talk*, and I rushed toward the entry door. One of the employees met up with me as I approached the door. I began to search my bag for my building key. As I shuffled my belongings in my bag, I whispered, "Hurry! Open this door! I am not ready for a convo with him!"

Gia said, "Okay, okay! I guess you are not on speaking terms."

I told her we were on break and I was not ready for a chat this early in the morning. Gia said she totally understood and sometimes it be like that. I knew Dean and I wouldn't speak for a while at least, but I never thought in a million years our relationship would just dissolve during a pandemic!

News media hit, and we were officially on lockdown! The number of deaths was climbing, and the spread of positive cases continued! People were hospitalized by the hour from difficulty of breathing, and the hospitals were running out of ventilators! We were officially in a worldwide pandemic from a fatal virus named COVID-19! We were led to believe the virus happened to evolve from an infected bat in a lab located in Wuhan, China. COVID-19 was found to have evolved from the SARS virus, and it spread quicker than we initially believed. The virus attacked the respiratory system, making it difficult for some to breathe. Soon after, we found the virus was soon confirmed to be airborne. Our state was officially on lockdown, and most people were told to work from home if they had the opportunity to do so. Nursing home deaths rose as the media spoke, and layoffs took off like wildfire. Businesses were forced to close unless you were essential, and schools went virtual. The world was in panic, and we all felt tremendous fear of the unknown. Nurses worked overtime and double-time just to keep their jobs and save lives. Violent riots continued all over the country and vandalism was inevitable. Our law enforcement members were attacked, and danger was bestowed upon them.

Our president stood strong while he was subjected to major criticism and blame for the country's current state. Still, Mr. President stood firm as he faced brutal attacks and mistreatment. The world was in disarray, and we heard more bad news over and over again on every news channel. Many people became depressed as we were forced to adjust as an entire nation, and no one could quite predict the outcome. We, as humans, lost that human touch and affection with each other.

Months passed. Still, we were forced to social-distance, wear a mask, and ordered to stay indoors unless for necessary purposes. Small businesses had to shut down due to the local restrictions mandated. Schools were shut down and later went virtual. Suicide rate amongst teenagers skyrocketed. Families were torn apart, and social distance with a mask on became the new normal. Holiday gatherings came to a halt, and some opted out of hosting any celebration at all. Our healthcare workers were honored as superheroes. Tokens of gratitude were shared with the entire healthcare community because most gave some but some gave their ALL!

Weddings were canceled, but graduation ceremonies continued at limited capacity. It was time for Andrew to say farewell to his high school class as we prepared for his next chapter. I had taken a few days off to make the trip down south to Andrew's college. The ride down was awesome! We listened to both country and rap music, and I was pleasantly surprised that Andrew developed a new skill of rapping! My phone rang, and it was a recruiter for a new job! I was super excited to begin my job search. Soon after, I received another call from a hiring manager for a lab local to my area. I was finally making progress and making connections! At the same time, Andrew and I were able to bond on a new level as I watched my son evolve into a man during such uncertain times. I helped Andrew move in and get settled while I enjoyed time away in beautiful weather from the everyday struggle back home. I also made a connection with a recruiter in Georgia, and life seemed to finally look a little brighter!

Morning came, and it was time to say goodbye to my baby boy. We had planned on meeting up at 10:00 a.m. before Andrew's orientation to say our last goodbyes. I received a text that read, "Where are you, Mom?"

I responded with, "Right around the corner, honey. Exactly where we planned to meet."

Andrew called my phone line, and when I picked up the line, he sounded as if he was could barely catch a breath! Oh no! Was everything okay?

Andrew shouted, "I think I will make it, so see you soon," and he hung up the line.

Not even two minutes later, I saw a very lean young man dart around the corner COMPLETELY out of breath.

"Oh my god, Mom," Andrew gasped. "I don't think I ever ran so fast in my life," he said as tears fell down his face.

I was completely choked up, and I gave Andrew the tightest hug as tears fell down my cheeks. This was my last goodbye to my son as he began a new chapter in his life. As I wiped my tears and looked into Andrew's eyes, I reminded him that he could always come home because he would always be welcomed with an open heart! Once again, I saw that childhood smile Andrew carried that lit up his face, and my heart smiled. I felt relieved that Andrew was settled in his new home. Andrew said he knew he could come home or transfer anytime, and we parted ways by reminding each other that we loved each other very much. I grabbed a tissue and ran out the front hotel to catch my cab. I had a flight to catch back home and I was running a little late! I started to hum a song in my head that brought me back to the days when Andrew was just a child and I had to leave occasionally on weekend trips for business.

> Leaving ona Jet Plane by John Denver
>
> All my bags are packed
> I'm ready to go
> I'm stand-in' here outside your door
> I hate to wake you unto say goodbye
> But the dawn is breakin'
> It's early morn
> The taxi's waitin'
> He's blowin' his horn
> Already I'm so lonesome
> I could die

So kiss me and smile for me
Tell me that you'll wait for me
Hold me like you'll never let me
   go
'Cause I'm leavin' on a jet plane
Don't know when I'll be back
   again
Oh, babe, I hate to go

Every place I go, I'll think of you
Every song I sing, I'll sing for you

Now the time has come to leave
   you
One more time
Let me kiss you
Then close your eyes
And I'll be on my way
Dream about the days to come
When I won't have to leave alone
About the times, I won't have to
   say

Kiss me and smile for me
Tell me that you'll wait for me
Hold me like you'll never let me
   go
'Cause I'm leavin' on a jet plane
Don't know when I'll be back
   again
Oh, babe, I hate to go

I flew back home to a lonely home with just me, myself, and I. Dean and I didn't make contact, but there were moments I wished we did. Although things were far from perfect, I still loved Dean. I thought about him often and wished him well. I had high hopes that time apart would do us both well. I felt lonely at times, and I missed the company by Dean, but my hurt lingered, and I wanted the tension at work to die down. I thought time would heal our pain and also give us the chance to reflect on our misunderstanding of each other. I was hoping we would overcome and grow closer someday if our love was strong enough. I was hopeful work would just STOP all the pain, tension, and worry they caused me. I needed my job, and I was committed to the people I helped and worked for.

Months passed, and we all adjusted to working at home. Technical difficulties somewhat subsided, but I still noticed red camera dots in my laptop as if someone was spying on me.

Tension died down, and the executive leadership team seemed more engaged. Communication tied together, and I felt hopeful. I was told I would be compensated fairly for the work I took on, and it felt satisfying. I even received an email from the BOSS Man owner. It was a response to a message I sent out to one of the executive leadership team members. I was shocked! I haven't heard any real communication in over a year! I was relieved to know my job may be secure after all. The next morning, I even received a text message on my company phone. Wow! Guess who? Boss Man was finally communicating with me again, and Dean and I were estranged for months. What a coincidence! We held a short conversation over Independence Day Holiday, and we even shared where we would share the holiday. I heard airplanes over my house, and there seemed to be a disconnect. The boss said he must have been in a bad area because his text sent out to me didn't go through, and he sent me the screenshot. I remembered hearing the boss bought a plane and took up flying as a hobby.

A few days passed, and I didn't hear from the boss and I sensed the tension returned. I finally caught on to what appeared to be an emotional trap. My search for a new job began, but it was conducted after work hours. There was a close eye kept on me while working from home, and there seemed to be pop-up meetings called by Kate without much notice. Finally, I became frustrated and didn't respond to a request as calmly as I normally would. I felt under constant attack, and I felt as if I just had enough. I was actively searching for a new job, but my time was still limited, and we were currently in a pandemic. Still, I searched and searched and applied to positions I found to be a good fit for.

Finally, a meeting was strung up on Friday at 4:00 p.m. via Zoom. I attended the call, not knowing it would be the end of a very long and dreadful chapter. The meeting called was just a way to find an excuse to fire me for no good reason and so it finally came to end.

Although I was relieved I would no longer be subjected to such odd behavior and mistreatment on a daily basis, I was left without a job during a REAL PANDEMIC! I wasn't even able to collect on extra funds due to COVID-19 like most. I was suddenly out of work because I was told the relationship just wasn't working out, and today would be my last day. I informed Kate that I knew it would come down to some excuse to let me go, but frankly, I was too tired and sick of the mistreatment; so I turned the ball back in her court and asked what the next step would be. I was hoping for an answer such as, "We will provide severance until you find other work or at least for a few months." NOT EVEN CLOSE! The response was extremely degrading after all the hard effort I placed into that organization.

Kate said, "We will offer you two weeks' severance if you would just confirm your email."

So I did confirm my email, but I was sure to contact my attorney to review the severance before I agreed or signed any document.

My mail became the highlight of my day. Packages were often sent to my address incorrectly, and I found myself delivering the mail to the correct address a few homes down. I made contact with the town post office, so they made a note of it; but still, some mail was received super late or not at all. Once again, I opened up a legal packet I wished I didn't. I was out of a job during a pandemic under extreme stress only to find that Joe filed another motion against me for residential custody and to eliminate support entirely for Andrew. At this point, I wasn't collecting support at all anyway nor was I collecting any funds for college so I was totally confused by the entire motion in itself. The only logical explanation was so Joe could attack me just one more time through the legal system. After all, what sense would it make to beat up on me while I was already down? It made total sense, and once again I was in another legal battle just to defend myself.

Months passed, and I had developed a slight depression. I lost sleep and battled UTIs from all the stress I faced. Once again, that feeling of loneliness appeared, and I wished I had my dad to lean on. I felt alone, scared, and worried about my future. I thought about contacting a therapist, but I didn't know who to contact. So I focused my energy on a full-force search for new employment, but my worry became heavy when thoughts of the same repetitive story struck again in a new workplace. Countless hours of sleep were lost, and I couldn't help but worry about how Andrew's tuition bill would be paid. I felt trapped within myself, and so I started to write my emotions down on paper during the interim of my job search. Still, I stayed the course and searched and searched until I finally found a new employer to play ball with me. After a total of four face-to-face rigorous interviews, I was offered a position as an operations lead. I finally was offered a salary I should have been making three years ago, but I had to start all over again. I had to adjust to an entirely new culture, new employees, and new computer systems, but there was a sign. On my final interview, I noticed a textbook placed in the lobby. I picked up the book while I was waiting only to notice the author had the same last name as I. I knew there was some reason for this next stop along my travels. Although once again, I had to prove to the leaders my capabilities, experience, skills, and commitment to the new organization I accepted a position with.

Projects were quickly thrown at me for completion with deadlines. I was under major pressure to complete tasks I had no real experience in! I could barely understand my boss's directives, and he wasn't so easy to contact. Oh my gosh! When my boss, and I finally made contact, the directives were short with minimal explanation because his time was limited and of the essence. I pondered if I was set up to fail or faced with a challenge to complete. Was this a way for my boss to make me quit, or was it his way of testing me? Either way, it was a MAKE-OR-BREAK situation and that I was determined to MAKE!

I started my day early in the office and stayed later than expected. I completed tasks I never knew of and felt more accomplished in two months than I did the last two years! I only had time for a quick bite after work and passed out early in the evenings. My weekends were consumed with errands I couldn't get to during the week. The holidays quickly approached, and there were more to-dos on my list. Text messages were nonstop, all day, and some were even ignored. One particular text came in the week after Thanksgiving…

Chapter 12

Guess Who's Back in Town?

The text read, "Hi. How are you? It's the Holidays and I wanted to reach out because we have a past."

I knew exactly who the messenger was before I even confirmed the name on my phone. My initial thought to myself was, *Yes. Oh yes, we certainly did have a past!* At that moment, I had mixed emotions. I was still angry and hurt we couldn't work out our disagreements like adults. I was still upset by the degrading comments thrown around, and the lack of will to apologize on Dean's behalf. I was still upset by the rage I witnessed during our arguments. I wasn't sure how to respond, but it was nice to hear some anger may have subsided. Time has healed, and Dean was okay. I knew Dean wasn't completely thrilled with my behavior either, but it was nice to know that I was thought of. I couldn't NOT respond at all because I was honestly glad to read the message and hear from Dean. But still, I knew the disagreements we had were a reality, so how would the relationship be any different now? I had flaws, too, and maybe thought too much. My response was, "Alive. I am alive, how are you?"

Dean responded with the same, "I am alive, too."

Dean and I agreed to connect and hopefully make amends. I was cautious of the virus, but Dean assured me we would be just fine. I invited Dean over for lunch since most small businesses were closed, and we were limited to dining.

Knock, knock… Guess who? It was Dean, just as handsome as he was when we drifted pre-COVID-19. Dean had a bouquet of flowers in his hands that I had a feeling may not have originally been purchased for me. In any event, I accepted the bouquet and placed them immediately in a vase with cold water in the center of my table in the same spot I always kept my floral arrangements from Dean. It was a post-Thanksgiving lunch without any noise. We talked about the pandemic for a while and shifted into our breakup. Although I was initially wary of making amends with Dean, I was quickly pleasantly surprised! I guess I should have never underestimated Big Dean when I assumed he had narcissistic characteristics. I just didn't think I would hear the word *sorry* or anything remotely close. I didn't think Dean was ready to assume any responsibility, but I was so relieved when I found out he did! Dean apologized, and I think I fell quicker than before! Just when I thought people didn't change… I realized they don't. Dean was Dean and I was I. People don't fully CHANGE or pull a 360.

It was at that very moment when I realized people shouldn't completely change! People shouldn't completely change their makeup or core because that is how God made them, and it is exactly how we are unique. People should only change what makes them feel unhappy about themselves! I realized change is within our very own control and we have the power to work on or improve what we want to change about ourselves. We, as couples, can come to a deeper understanding and improve our communication with each other, but it is not our right to demand complete change on our partner when they are the exact same person we formed a love with.

Better get the wine because Dean didn't change, but he was definitely back…better than before!

I also admitted my flaws for my constant and deep thoughts, and we both realized that we still loved each other and our love never died.

> Tale as old as time…
> True as it can be
> Barely even friends
> Then somebody bends
> Unexpectedly
>
> Just a little change
> Small, to say the least
> Both a little scared
> Neither one prepared
> Beauty and the Beast

Ever just the same
And ever a surprise, yeah
Ever as before
And ever just as sure
As the sun will rise,
Oh, oh, oh
Tale as old as time
Tune as old as song
Bittersweet and strange
Finding you can change
Learning you were wrong

Certain as the Sun
Certain as the Sun
Rising in the east
Tale as old as time
Song as old as rhyme
Beauty and the Beast
Woah

Beauty and the Beast
Beauty and the Beast
Released by Walt Disney Records

Dean and I decided to take things slow until we were solid enough with our relationship and the direction it was heading in. Besides, we were also in a world-spread pandemic, so what was the rush? The world was still, and all was calm, with not many in sight. We were currently in a very important presidential election. Christmas was around the corner, and we couldn't help but spend the night together. Dean and I exchanged gifts, enjoyed a turkey dinner, and a glass of Cabernet on a cold winter's evening. Dean and I had a lot to catch up on, but we always enjoyed each other's company. Andrew was soon off to college, and Dean and I would soon finally be able to enjoy our time alone! We were soon approaching a New Year. Although the challenges remained, it felt like we were entering a new chapter—but a very important or life-altering chapter.

HAPPY NEW YEAR! Dean and I had shared a toast of champagne and strawberries together. It was a new year, and although the challenges were still existent, something felt very different. Was it because I was now employed in a new organization? Was it because I no longer had to worry about all the renovations in my home? Was it because my family and I were still so close but somewhat distant and apart. Was it because the world was still? Was it because we had adjusted to the new normal of social distancing and wearing masks? Was it the overwhelming fear bestowed upon us? Maybe it was the peace deep within Dean and I finally felt in our relationship. We didn't have the distractions we once did. I didn't have to worry about dinner for my child in the home as I once did. We didn't have to worry about our privacy as Dean and I once did. Dean and I didn't have to sacrifice our time as we once did. It was time for Tania and Dean to enjoy couple time together—alone—and we did just that between different shades of gray walls.

Our love became more passionate than ever, and I thought of the movie *Fifty Shades of Grey*. I found myself under Dean's spell, submissive to his sexual demands; only this time, it was more loving, trusting, respectful, and passionate. There seemed to have been more respect and trust built since our time away, and you could feel it during our most intimate moments. I was completely in love with Dean, and he was also reassured. I finally accepted that there wasn't a better partner out there for me, and Dean was everything and all I would ever need. I finally met my soulmate, the man of my visions. It was so surreal yet so real. I was finally home in Dean's arms safe and sound. My journey was far from over because life just began. It was real! Although it will never be perfect, I found romantic love with a partner could work out if two people want it to. Romantic love or any form of love really does exist for all those that believe it does! It almost felt as if we rose even higher. I knew Dean and I both carried a higher level of our faith in the love we had for each other because when the odds were against us, our hearts never gave up. Our love stood strong, stronger than ever before. My past and the pain I once carried seemed to subside, and I was so excited to begin a new life with my forever-lasting love, Dean Michael. I couldn't believe it was happening! I was reminded of the rose Dean bought me for our first Valentine's Day together and the song by Bette Midler I once sang years ago.

The Rose

Some say love, it is a river
That drowns the tender reed
Some say love, it is a razor
That leaves your soul to bleed.
Some say love, it is a hunger
An endless aching need
I say love, it is a flower
And you, its only seed

It's the heart, afraid of breaking
That never learns to dance
It's the dream, afraid of waking
That never takes the chance
It's the one who won't be taken
Who cannot seem to give
And the soul, afraid of dying

That never learns to live.
When the night has been too
    lonely
And the road has been too long
And you think that love is only
For the lucky and the strong
Just remember in the winter
Far beneath the bitter snows
Lies the seed that with the sun's
    love
In the spring becomes the rose.

I finally accepted that love isn't perfect, and it has no rules. Love can sometimes come and go in and out of our lives and sometimes last for a lifetime. At times, love can disappoint us because it might disappear too soon. At other times, love can last longer in our lives and truly surprise us! Whatever amount of love enters our lives, it is a virtue and a true blessing to experience any form. Love is real! Just as hate is alive and a real emotion, so is love. The beauty of love is that it can weaken hatred. We have the power within ourselves to give and show others love to those we so desire to.

Although the legal battle continued with Joe, Dean was there to support me through it all. My fears subsided through the love Dean provided and both love and strength God continued to provide me. Dean and I finally moved past all the fears and anxieties we once shared. We still had our differences, but we learned to accept and love each other for who we are. We were on a new journey of peace, love, and self-fulfillment together...hopefully forever, but I know one must find self-acceptance and love within him/herself before a lasting love with a partner could exist.

About the Author

A. Maksimow was born and raised in New Jersey. A college graduate of Rutgers University with a passion to create and inspire, A. Maksimow was always fond of the English language and romance stories as a young girl, but she didn't develop a desire to write until her middle age. Philosophy has been by far A. Maksimow 's  greatest study of interest, and she continues to learn and improve from her experiences.

A. Maksimow is a professional and mother to one child, son Jakob. Although A. Maksimow has only one child of her own, she has a sincere love for all children and animals, but she can easily find beauty in all. A. Maksimow enjoys spending time with her family and friends when she is not in deep focus, writing down her thoughts. A. Maksimow loves nature, and she appreciates the natural beauty and serenity it has to offer. Cooking, Pilates, and travel are just a few of A. Maksimow's favorites.

Although A. Maksimow is a first-time author, she looks forward to developing greater skill in writing in her sequel as she continues to write from her heart and inspire others.